HARLEQUIN®
Presents

The last, hazy days of August are meant for basking
in the sun and reading good books. Whether you're
relaxing in your backyard, on your porch or maybe
chilling on vacation, make sure to have a selection of
Harlequin Presents titles by your side. We've got eight
great novels to choose from....

Bestselling author Lynne Graham presents her latest tale
of a mistress who's forced to marry an Italian billionaire
in *Mistress Bought and Paid For*. And Miranda Lee is as
steamy as ever with her long-awaited romp, *Love-Slave
to the Sheikh*, for our hot UNCUT miniseries.

You never know what goes on behind closed doors,
and we have three very different stories about
marriages to prove it: Anne Mather's sexy and emotional
Jack Riordan's Baby will have your heart in your mouth
while also tugging at its strings, while *Bought by Her
Husband,* Sharon Kendrick's newest release, and
Kate Walker's *The Antonakos Marriage* are two slices
of Greek tycoon heaven with spicy twists!

If it's something more traditional you're after, we've
plenty of choice: *By Royal Demand,* the first installment
in Robyn Donald's new regal saga, THE ROYAL HOUSE
OF ILLYRIA, won't disappoint. Or you might like to try
The Italian Millionaire's Virgin Wife by Diana Hamilton
and *His Very Personal Assistant* by Carole Mortimer—
two shy, sensible, prim-and-proper women find
themselves living lives they've never dreamed of when
they attract two rich, arrogant and darkly handsome
men!

Enjoy!

Mama Mia!

Harlequin Presents®

ITALIAN HUSBANDS

They're tall, dark—and ready to marry!

If you love marriage-of-convenience stories that ignite into marriages of passion, then look no further. We've got the heroes you love to read about and the women who tame them.

Watch for more exciting tales of romance, Italian-style!

Available only from Harlequin Presents®!

Diana Hamilton

THE ITALIAN MILLIONAIRE'S VIRGIN WIFE

ITALIAN HUSBANDS

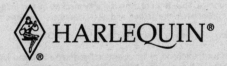

HARLEQUIN®

TORONTO • NEW YORK • LONDON
AMSTERDAM • PARIS • SYDNEY • HAMBURG
STOCKHOLM • ATHENS • TOKYO • MILAN • MADRID
PRAGUE • WARSAW • BUDAPEST • AUCKLAND

If you purchased this book without a cover you should be aware that this book is stolen property. It was reported as "unsold and destroyed" to the publisher, and neither the author nor the publisher has received any payment for this "stripped book."

ISBN-13: 978-0-373-12558-6
ISBN-10:   0-373-12558-5

THE ITALIAN MILLIONAIRE'S VIRGIN WIFE

First North American Publication 2006.

Copyright © 2005 by Diana Hamilton.

All rights reserved. Except for use in any review, the reproduction or utilization of this work in whole or in part in any form by any electronic, mechanical or other means, now known or hereafter invented, including xerography, photocopying and recording, or in any information storage or retrieval system, is forbidden without the written permission of the publisher, Harlequin Enterprises Limited, 225 Duncan Mill Road, Don Mills, Ontario, Canada M3B 3K9.

All characters in this book have no existence outside the imagination of the author and have no relation whatsoever to anyone bearing the same name or names. They are not even distantly inspired by any individual known or unknown to the author, and all incidents are pure invention.

This edition published by arrangement with Harlequin Books S.A.

® and TM are trademarks of the publisher. Trademarks indicated with ® are registered in the United States Patent and Trademark Office, the Canadian Trade Marks Office and in other countries.

www.eHarlequin.com

Printed in U.S.A.

All about the author...
Diana Hamilton

DIANA HAMILTON lives with her husband in a beautiful part of Shropshire, an idyll shared with two young Cavalier King Charles spaniels and a cat. Her three children and their assorted offspring are frequent visitors. When she's not writing Presents books, she's driving her sports car—and frightening the locals—pottering in the garden or lazing in the sun on the terrace beneath a ridiculous hat and reading.

Diana has been fascinated by the written word from an early age and she firmly believes she was born with her nose in a book.

After leaving grammar school she studied fine art, but put her real energy into gaining her advertising copywriting degree and worked as a copywriter until her family moved to a remote part of Wales, where her third child was born. Four years later they returned to Shropshire, where they have been ever since, gradually restoring the rambling Elizabethan manor that Diana gave her heart to on sight. In the mid-seventies Diana took up her pen again and over the following ten years she combined writing thirty novels for Robert Hale of London with raising her children and the ongoing restoration work.

In 1987 Diana realized her dearest ambition—the publication of her first Harlequin romance. She had come home. And that warm feeling persists to this day as over forty-five Presents novels later she is still in love with the genre.

CHAPTER ONE

ANDREO PASCALI, cursing the day the admirable Knox had left his employ, taking retirement to make her home with her recently widowed sister in Kent, impatiently lifted the final sheet of paper, scanned it in a nanosecond and even more impatiently tossed it aside.

'No details,' he dismissed tersely, his wide sensual mouth tightening with annoyance, lancing a look of displeasure at his current lover.

Though current was on the verge of becoming past. Trisha was becoming far too demanding and clingy— definitely against his emphatically stated ground rules.

Only last evening he'd returned from the agency with the intention of wrestling with the problem of how to come up with an idea for a sensational TV commercial, one bearing the inimitable Pascali stamp of excellence and selling clout for something as deeply uninspiring as a brand of ready meals, only to find that Trisha had let herself in and was waiting for him with a wretched Chinese takeaway festering in the oven. She'd done that fluffing up thing with her hair, accompanying it with the usual pouty mouth bit—once sexily amusing but now utterly boring— and had told him, sounding deadly serious, 'What you need, light of my life, is a wife. Then you wouldn't be facing these dreary interviews and wasting the time you say is so precious.'

His scowl darkened. As a hint, it seriously raised his annoyance threshold. She knew darn well he didn't need or want a wife. He wanted an unobtrusive housekeeper and at this rate it didn't look as if he was going to get one!

'The last two girls seemed perfectly fine,' he snapped. 'Though, I grant you, the first applicant was a nightmare.' Eighty if she was a day, even though her letter of application had given her age as fifty, dotty as they came. He'd had Trisha make her a cup of tea and had personally put her into a taxi. She'd given the address of a retirement home to the driver and waved maniacally as she'd been driven away.

'There was nothing wrong with the other two,' he reiterated tightly. Vital energy, constrained for too long, had him on his feet, pacing the confines of his home office. 'Good qualifications, excellent references,' he reminded with a bite.

'Darling,' Trisha soothed with a sycophantic smile. 'Don't get cross. I offered my help and advice when you said you didn't do domestic stuff. And my advice is that both those girls wouldn't stay for longer than a few weeks. Reasonably bright, passably pretty, leave to get married in no time. You need a middle-aged home body. And there are no details because she didn't send a letter of application; she simply phoned yesterday afternoon and asked for an interview.'

Had sounded bossy, too. Andreo wouldn't find bossiness in the least bit sexy. Whereas either of the previous two...

And having seen her when admitting her to Andreo's darling home, and again when seeing the third applicant out, she'd reached the conclusion that Mercy Howard would do very nicely. Twenty-two years old, so sadly not middle-aged, but plain as a house brick and decidedly, wholesomely dumpy—no competition. Beginning to feel on shaky ground herself, she didn't want the complications of round the clock competition. Andreo never gave a thought to marriage. Before the start of their relationship he'd stated that he didn't do long-term stuff. She'd gone along with that. Well, she'd have been a fool to throw a spanner in the works at that stage. Her sole aim was to make him change his mind, decide he wanted her as his wife, setting her up for a life of ease and giving her access to untold wealth.

No, the woman who didn't find Andreo Pascali's perfect bone structure, tall lean physique and dark charismatic Latin looks seriously lust-worthy—not to mention his wildly impressive bank account—was yet to be born. The Howard female wouldn't be any different, but darling Andreo wouldn't be remotely tempted to take any notice of her no doubt clumsy attempts to hit on him.

'You might as well see her since she's here,' Trisha cooed, running her fingers through his midnight hair. 'You never know, she could well be just what we're looking for.'

Disliking the proprietorial 'we' bit and even more disliking the impression of being humoured, Andreo jerked his head away, stiffened his impressive shoulders and positioned himself behind his desk again, a massive frown bringing his brows down in two straight black bars. Trisha's time was definitely up. He'd have his PA select a suitably expensive piece of jewellery and deliver it to her apartment first thing in the morning accompanied by his standard note saying farewell and no regrets.

And, unless the fourth applicant was over eighty and completely doolally, the job was hers. He had important creative work to get stuck into.

The moment she'd found the address she was looking for, Mercy had felt horrible qualms. A converted warehouse in one of the trendiest Thames-side areas was hardly the right setting for a humble country bumpkin. How often had Carly teased, 'Get street-wise, kid,' when she'd confessed to being appalled, mystified or downright scared of the frenetic life of this great cosmopolitan city? Despite being in London for two years, she was still an old-fashioned country vicar's daughter at heart with old-fashioned values and a yearning for the much slower pace of life she'd been used to.

But she had determination on her side and, clutching her large shabby handbag, had marched up to the fine wooden door, pressing a bell. Startled by a voice issuing from some sort of discreet metal contraption, she had obeyed instructions and given her name and business.

Eventually the door had swung open as if by magic and she'd found herself walking into a huge vestibule, the ceiling of which soared three storeys high, with a staircase winding up and leading to balustraded floors. To be met by a big-haired blonde of such magnificent proportions, shown to full advantage by pink harem pants and a toning glittery, clingy top, that Mercy had immediately felt like a small fat grey mouse, her modest five-three seeming to diminish to a mere inch or two.

. Consulting a clipboard, the blonde had announced, 'You must be Ms Howard.' A wide white smile followed a minute scrutiny of her less than flattering boxy grey suit, sensible shoes and unwieldy handbag. 'I'm Signor Pascali's—' the coy arching of one artfully darkened brow, followed by a huskily stressed '—friend.' A meaningful simper, then, 'He is interviewing at the moment, so if you'd like to take a seat I'm sure he won't keep you waiting for too long.'

The leather and chrome seat she located beside a glass-topped table was surprisingly comfortable. But Mercy couldn't relax even though she planted her feet together and cradled her comfy old handbag on her lap. The qualms had begun first thing this morning when Carly had gleefully apprised her of the exact identity of her hoped-for future employer.

'I sat up half the night on the net researching the guy. Get this—he's a living legend and he's only thirty-one! He owns, directs and literally is the creative genius behind the Pascali Ad Agency. Worth billions in his own right, not counting a load of family dosh. His main home is here in London—presumably where you'll be working and living—plus he owns a villa near Amalfi and an apartment in Rome. Interested in modern art. No wife and kids, so there won't be much for you to do other than flick a duster over his Picassos and Hockneys!' Shrugging into the navy tailored suit jacket, the one with a discreet embroidered logo of the world-famous cosmetic company she worked for on the narrow lapel, the dark colour of the sleek fabric drawing attention to her enviably straight jaw-length ash-blonde bob, she blew Mercy a kiss. 'Must dash before I'm late again. And the best of luck—and remember, you've got a beautiful smile, so use it a lot!'

Bleary-eyed from lack of sleep, having been up most of the night cleaning offices, which was increasingly the only type of work the domestic agency found for her because, according to one of her workmates, she was always reliable, thorough and never ever called in sick, she had found it impossible to grab the customary two hours or so of rest, getting more and more het up about the coming interview.

Coming across the job vacancy as she'd browsed through an up-market magazine while waiting for a routine six-monthly dental check-up yesterday lunchtime, it had seemed that her guardian angel was working overtime on her behalf. A live-in housekeeper was required for an Andreo Pascali, the salary quoted large enough to make her eyes pop out of her head.

On that kind of money, no living expenses—and presumably she'd be fed as well as housed—she could do a huge amount to help her brother James through his medical training, far more than she was managing at the moment even though she scraped together every penny that wasn't needed for her share of the rent and food.

Hopelessly impractical where money matters were concerned, he'd feel utterly at sea if he finished his gruelling training—and already he was talking about eventually going on to take a higher degree in surgery—and woke up to the fact that he was saddled with a mountainous student debt.

Convinced that the job vacancy she'd happened across had been heaven-sent, she'd phoned and stated—well, more demanded, she recollected with a flush of discomfiture—that she needed an appointment for an interview. It had all seemed to fit so perfectly, given that only the day before Carly had dropped her bombshell.

The old school friend she'd shared the tiny flat with for the last two years was moving out, moving in with her boyfriend, marriage definitely on the cards.

She'd been genuinely happy for her, of course she had. How could she be otherwise when Carly had been so good to her? Two years ago, days after her twentieth birthday, she'd been at her wits' end, stricken with grief at the death of her remaining parent, not knowing how she would manage to help her brilliant brother through his long years of training and exist on her odd job earnings now that her mother's church pension had died with her.

Leaving school herself at sixteen on the death of her father, she'd agreed with her mother that it was her duty to earn something to put by for her much brighter younger brother's education. She'd taken any work she could find in the village where the family had moved from the vicarage to live in a small cottage owned by the church authorities which was a guaranteed home for their mother's lifetime.

Times had been hard but contented. She'd been planning to work full-time towards a qualification in catering and housecraft to open up a future of professional housekeeping or, more adventurously, starting up her own business catering for private dinner parties and weddings. That ambition had been put on hold but, even so, she had enjoyed the work she did find. Cleaning, tidying gardens, shopping for the housebound, dog-walking.

It had been Carly who'd stepped in at that worrisome time. She worked as a beautician in a swanky London store and had offered, 'You can share with me. The flat's not much bigger than a shoe box but we'd manage. You could share the rent so you'd be doing me a favour. And there are loads of domestic agencies just crying out for recruits. I could fix up some interviews. Okay?'

So she'd got a home and a job and her father's spinster aunt, a retired schoolmistress, had offered James a home during his vacations. A quiet Cornish village where he could revise and study in peace and quiet before returning to the famous London teaching hospital for his next term of training.

Now, as the statuesque blonde escorted a tall, graceful, fine-featured brunette—probably with a whole pile of qualifications tucked up in her smart leather shoulder purse—over to the front door, telling her, 'You will be contacted within the next day or two to let you know whether you are on the short list,' Mercy's spirits dropped through the soles of her brown lace-ups. She felt totally out of place.

And if that with-it, confident-looking woman might not even make a short list, what hope had she? And had been left for a further ten minutes to stew, torn between the desire to slope away, advertise for someone prepared to share the tiny flat when Carly moved out at the end of the week and carry on as before, scratching to save every penny she could, and the need to tough it out, give it her best shot. After all, she had nothing to lose except the tube fare.

Still dithering, the decision to flee or fight was taken out of her hands when the blonde bombshell beckoned from the doorway of the room she'd previously entered on the far side of the vast vestibule.

Heart thumping at the base of her throat, Mercy rose to her feet, wishing she'd at least had something more impressive to wear than the sober and sensible suit that had been bought for her father's funeral all those years ago.

But then she heartened herself by deciding that 'sensible' would be a quality any employer would look for in a housekeeper, so sensible and practical was the way she would pitch it. A girl didn't have to be a vision of loveliness to wash dishes and polish floors, did she?

And the legendary, super well-heeled Signor Pascali was only a human being, just as she was, wasn't he?

But there were human beings and human beings was her first insane thought when the too-handsome-by-a-country-mile specimen viewed her dumpy personage across the cluttered expanse of his desk.

His lean, strong face was taut with barely concealed impatience and there was an aura of predatory stillness about the honed, whiplash tight, power-packed frame that suggested a tendency to leap on anyone who stepped out of line and tear them apart limb from limb.

The dark grey eyes continued to assess her until she felt like squirming through the floorboards. His eyes spoke of a vital volatility, though, and that eased her somewhat because if he really was a creative genius then he probably wasn't noticing the toffee-coloured corkscrew curls that made her look as if she'd been in a wind tunnel for hours no matter how hard she tried to tame them, or her plain face. He was probably miles away on some fantastically creative plane or other.

But the comforting illusion was shattered when those eyes finally got down as far as her clumpy shoes. A terse hand movement gestured her to take the hot seat opposite him and he simultaneously turned to his hovering blonde 'friend'.

'I need coffee, Trisha. Now.' He would conduct this final interview on his own, without annoying twittered interruptions regarding qualifications, experience, references. He'd wasted too much time already.

Sensing a reluctance, he added, 'And a cup for—' he consulted a sheet of paper '—Ms Mercy Howard.'

The command, delivered in that slightly accented rough velvet voice had the blonde—Trisha—scurrying away, Mercy noted, an odd squirmy feeling starting up inside her as her eyes homed in on his wide, sensual mouth. Never having thought of any part of any male before in those terms, it gave her a decidedly peculiar feeling.

With his about to be ex-lover out of the way, Andreo lounged back in his chair and regarded the final applicant from beneath lowered lids, not prepared to waste a moment more of his valuable time. He had two options. Contact either one of the two earlier candidates and offer the job or hire this one.

His smoky eyes narrowed further. He took advice from no one, but in this case maybe Trisha did have a point, he reluctantly conceded. Both of the other two women had been lookers, beautifully turned out and groomed, self-assured and confident in themselves. Hire one of them and wait to see how long it would take for her to persuade some poor sucker to slip a plain gold band on her wedding finger.

Then he'd have to go through this whole charade again.

With this one he wouldn't run nearly the same risk, he decided. A plump no-nonsense—apart from her weird hair—little personage, the only sign of discomfiture showing in her rapidly pinkening unremarkable face.

The job was hers.

'Experience of running a household?' he barked out. Better go through some of the motions. Unless some serious flaw was unearthed, he had another housekeeper after two irritating weeks without one. His life would go on as before, letting him concentrate on what was important without having to bother about tiresome domestic matters like finding clean socks and figuring out how to make a decent cup of coffee.

Mercy breathed a short sigh of relief. The way he'd been looking at her, as if she were a previously undiscovered life form, had seriously unnerved her. Clasping her hands together, she answered in a rush. 'I ran my mother's household for four years, plus holding down several part-time jobs. And I began studying catering and housecraft at night school, but had to—' About to explain the circumstances that had led to her abandoning the course, namely her mother's deteriorating health, she found herself robbed of speech when Signor Pascali slotted in, 'Boyfriends?'

Her mouth falling open as she swallowed her words, Mercy floundered. What had that to do with her ability to housekeep? 'No,' she finally answered when the impatient tightening of his mouth indicated that he'd waited too long for a response he'd expected to receive at the double.

'Any family commitments?' Then, as if the question needed elaboration, 'Any children? Aged relatives with health or drink problems who will expect you to drop everything and deal with regular minor emergencies?'

Mercy stiffened, primming her innocent of make-up full lips. Despite his devastating looks, this man was a bully. Time to stand up for herself; she probably wouldn't make the short list in any case.

'Signor Pascali, my father was a man of the cloth. Apart from a sip of Communion wine, alcohol never crossed his lips. My mother was a gentle soul who never once made an unreasonable demand. Sadly, they are both gone. I do have a great-aunt in robust health and, as she lives in Cornwall, I'm hardly likely to rush to her side should she have the misfortune to suffer a head cold—not that she would dream of expecting me to. And, as for children, of course I don't have any. I am unmarried.'

'The unmarried state doesn't necessarily indicate the absence of offspring, in my experience,' he remarked in what she considered to be deep cynicism, but his sudden grin splintered her prickly mood, rendering him so handsome it made her eyes water. And he had laughing eyes, she noted, quite transfixed as he shot forward in his seat with an excess of energy, briefly consulting the sheet of paper on the desk in front of him, complacently reflecting that as a vicar's daughter she would probably have old fashioned moral values and be unlikely to do drugs or throw wild parties during his occasional absences.

'If you accept the position, Howard, you will have your own suite of rooms which you will keep to when off duty. You will manage all domestic matters unobtrusively. I do not wish to be informed or consulted on such trifles. For example, should a water pipe spring a leak you will contact a plumber and get it fixed without bothering me. You will deal with my laundry—I use two shirts a day. I rise at six-thirty and breakfast at eight after my usual run and shower. I rarely spend the evenings at home but when I intend to you will be notified and will prepare a meal for nine o'clock. On the occasions when I entertain, whether *à deux* or a dinner party for up to twenty you will contact the firm of caterers I always use and make all the necessary arrangements. And if I have an overnight guest then her requirements will be conveyed to you. Any questions?'

Mercy snatched in a ragged breath. Was it possible that he was about to offer her the job? It would be a life-saver! Her mind churning, her eyes widening as she struggled to come up with something both pertinent and sensible to ask him, not a single thing occurred to her except a disapproving need to know if the overnighting female guest was always the big blonde or whether he liked to ring the changes. And, as that would mark her down as being unbearably prissy, she was reduced to shaking her head and giving him a breathy 'No, I don't think so.' Gathering herself and thankfully finding a competent tone from somewhere, she tacked on, 'It seems quite straightforward.'

Plainly keen, Andreo decided. None of the usual questions about days off or holiday entitlement. His mind made up, he smiled into a pair of startlingly blue eyes. He leaned back, his indolent pose at odds with his driven inner need to be done with the whole business, see a housekeeper installed right now and wash his hands of the horrifying range of chores needed to ensure a smooth-running domestic life that had so unexpectedly loomed up since Knox had so inconveniently retired.

'Welcome on board, Howard.' He rose, his height and the intimidating breadth of his dark-shirted shoulders looming over her, a strong, finely made hand extended. 'You take up your duties as of tomorrow.'

Mercy's poleaxed gaze flicked up from that extended hand to lock with those dark pewter eyes. She'd got the peach of a job! Just like that! Her soft mouth dropped open then firmed decisively as she told him, 'Thank you. However, I can't possibly begin tomorrow.'

'And why not?' emerged on a bite as he dropped back into his seat at speed, his classic features hardening.

He was going to be a handful, Mercy labelled, refusing to quail beneath all that feature-darkening displeasure. Plainly he was used to getting all his own way. It was about time that someone taught him that life wasn't like that. Despite her self-acknowledged unprepossessing mousy appearance and her willingness to bend over backwards to help everyone, she was capable of putting her foot down if circumstances warranted it.

Giving him a moment to stew, she told him firmly, 'I am presently employed through a domestic agency. I am required to give a full week's notice. Of course I could merely leave and sacrifice a week's wages—which I would expect you to reimburse. But I never go back on a commitment. I would be happy to take up the position when I've served my notice,' she enforced, desperately hoping that she hadn't blown it.

Andreo's intimidating frown dissolved. The most glamorous, self-assured females around had been known to fall over backwards in their desire to comply with his slightest wishes, but now he'd been put in his place by a frumpy little glorified char-lady who should, by rights, have been willing to tie herself in knots in order to secure such a highly paid position. It was a novel experience and one which set his mouth twitching.

The twitch grew to a full blown grin as he shot to his feet. 'Then I'll expect you to take up your duties in one week, Howard. When the coffee finally arrives would you ask to be shown over the property?' Long legs propelled him towards the door. At least she'd proved she had integrity, he excused his uncharacteristic acceptance of non-compliance to his dictates, his mind sharply dismissing her and homing in on the work awaiting him at the agency.

Still reeling from the effect of that devastating smile, plus her good fortune in landing the job, Mercy composed herself to wait. The legendary Andreo Pascali wasn't as intimidating as she'd feared he would be.

Not if he was handled firmly.

CHAPTER TWO

THE alarm woke Mercy at six-thirty. She lay for a moment luxuriating in the blissful comfort of the huge double bed in the housekeeper's suite on the top floor of the conversion, enjoying both the April dawn light as it filtered through the gauzy white curtains at the large windows and the squirmy, excited feeling which was occupying the pit of her tummy.

Her new boss rose at this hour and breakfasted at eight. She would show him what she was capable of. She had seen him only briefly as she'd arrived yesterday morning. He'd let her in, shooting a penetrating look at his watch, not seeming to actually see her as he'd stated, 'Punctual. Good. I'll be out all day, Howard. I won't need a meal this evening. Settle yourself in and make the laundry your priority.'

Watching him stride away, hailing the taxi that seemed to appear by magic, she had marvelled, wide-eyed, at the excess of vitality that emanated from that tall frame, the sober, exquisitely tailored business suit at odds with all that barely leashed raw physical energy. Then she'd dragged her gaze away and had turned to begin her first day in his employ.

She'd really enjoyed it too, Mercy reflected as she rolled out of bed and headed for the *en suite* bathroom. She'd had the fantastic place to herself—not a sign of the blonde bombshell—and had hustled around really making herself useful.

Mildly tutting as she'd collected the garments strewn all over the bedroom and bathroom he occupied on the floor below hers, sorting the coloureds from the whites in the laundry room, her face had grown hot at the intimacy.

Too silly.

While they'd been at home together she'd done James's laundry, so she was well acquainted with male underwear. Though her brother's things hadn't sported labels bearing the names of top designers. So no need for her to get all hot under the collar, was there?

Shelving that recollection, she hoped he'd noticed the shirts hanging in pristine perfection in his vast wardrobe, the fact that his bedlinen had been changed, his bedroom dusted and vacuumed to within an inch of its life, and buttoned herself into one of the pale grey overalls she'd found lying on her bed, still in cellophane wrappers awaiting her arrival. She hoped so. She really did need to impress him with her quiet efficiency. She had to hang on to this job. She had spent the fifteen minutes she'd allowed herself for a lunch break yesterday working out just how much more she would be able to pay into her brother's bank account.

The resulting sum had made her hug herself with glee.

Tying her unruly, crinkly hair out of the way into two bunches—it was so thick and wild that one ponytail bunch wouldn't cut it—she decided that whoever had ordered her overalls must have had a grossly inflated idea of her size, then dismissed the thought as vanity because what she looked like—the side of a house—didn't matter one iota. All that mattered was that she impress her boss with her housekeeping skills.

By the time she heard the whirlwind that heralded his return from his morning run and his entry into the shower room off the entrance vestibule she had laid a single place setting at the starkly modern dining table that would seat twenty with comfort and was mentally setting aside something from her more than generous wages for the purchase of flowers to soften the severely masculine ambience of smoothly polished wooden floors and austere white walls which were adorned with a couple of oil paintings she couldn't make head nor tail of.

Fifteen minutes to eight. Shooting through to the state of the art kitchen, she had breakfast ready by eight on the dot and tracked him down to the room where she'd been interviewed. Standing just inside the door while he finished his call, which consisted of him telling someone he wouldn't reconsider and that was final, she was wondering if the correct procedure would be to smartly absent herself when Andreo ended the call, dropped his mobile into the clutter on his desk and, his face a picture of aggravation, demanded, 'Well?'

'Breakfast is ready, sir,' Mercy announced dispassionately. On what he was paying her she could afford to overlook snippy behaviour. Obviously, whoever he'd been talking to had rattled his cage and she just happened to be on the receiving end of the fallout.

Spectacular dark eyes dropped to her empty hands. 'I don't see it.'

Momentarily distracted by the way the morning

light touched the gleaming luxuriance of his dark hair
and emphasised the heart-stopping planes and hollows
of his amazing Latin looks, Mercy could only stare,
her soft mouth dropping open until she remembered
that rudely gawping wasn't exactly the on-the-ball behaviour expected of a super-efficient employee.

'The dining room, sir,' she put in rapidly, at pains
now to project effortless competence to make up for
that dismaying lapse, essayed a slight smile, opened
the door and stood aside for her boss to precede her.

Only he didn't.

'I take it in here,' was his quelling rejoinder. Then
that knock-'em-dead smile had her melting all over
as he amended, 'Sorry, Howard. You weren't to know
that, were you? Knox should have left you precise
instructions—' Then, his smile fading at the speed of
light, he reached for his trilling mobile, snatched it
up and spoke in a voice like ice daggers. 'I don't do
patience; you should know that. If you call this number one more time I shall have you prosecuted for
harassment.'

Mercy scurried, her face pink. How awful! If he
talked to her like he'd spoken to the unfortunate on
the other end of the phone she would curl up and die!
Or, more likely, ask him who he thought he was talking to and get the sack! He obviously had no inhibitions about bawling out anyone who displeased him.
She would have to watch her step and then some or
she might find herself and her meagre belongings
ejected straight out of the front door.

Finding the largest tray the kitchen had to offer,
she loaded it with Andreo's breakfast things and tottered back to his study. She would have to clear a

space on that immense cluttered desk. Really, she thought, out of breath with her exertions as she thrust the study door open with her hip, it would be far more convenient if he ate in the dining room. But it wasn't her place to tell him so. He paid her wages; he was, she supposed, entitled to call the tune.

He was intent on what he was doing, keying text into a computer housed on a work station at the far end of the room. Mercy placed the loaded tray on the floor while she cleared a space on his desk, hefted it into position and announced briskly, 'Your breakfast, sir.'

'So?' He sounded abstracted, on another planet. Then exasperation crept in. 'Bring it here, woman.'

Mercy ground her teeth together. Give me strength! was the plea that sprang to her lips, successfully smothered by her almost level, 'There isn't enough room on that bench, sir.'

She saw the wide shoulders stiffen beneath the crisp pale blue shirt he was wearing tucked into immaculately tailored narrow fitting dark grey trousers. 'Not room?' He turned to glare at her disbelievingly, then got to his feet in one fluid movement, his magnificent eyes landing on a plate of eggs sunny side up, grilled bacon and tomatoes, a rack of toast, butter dish, honey, the teapot and accessories.

Andreo felt his face go blank as he briefly closed his eyes and swallowed the impulse to shout, You're fired! Knox plainly hadn't done as he'd instructed and made a list of all his requirements to leave for her successor.

His voice gritty with the determination to be even-handed, he stated, 'There are things you should know,

Howard. I'm busy and about to get busier. I don't have time to eat my way through enough to feed a small army. I simply require a cup of strong, un-sweetened black coffee—nothing else—on the dot of eight before I leave for my place of work at eight-ten.' Making a huge production of it, he consulted the wafer-thin platinum watch on his wrist and pointed out drily, 'It is already eight-fifteen. And I do not need or want a heart attack on a plate. Take it away!'

Mercy drew herself up to her unimpressive full height and shot him a look of mild disapproval. During her odd job days when her mother had been alive, she had often looked after Mrs Fletcher's two-year-old strong willed son and could recognise the onset of a temper tantrum with the best of them.

Sure of her ground, she pointed out with the breezy firmness tantrums demanded, 'It is good wholesome food. Bacon and eggs once in a while did no one any harm. Having just black coffee to start the day on—' she made a tutting noise '—won't do at all. Breakfast is the most important meal of the day, and while I'm employed to look after you and your home a decent breakfast is what you'll get. Eat it before it goes cold.'

Then, belatedly reminding herself of her subservient position and her need to hold on to it, she tacked on, 'Will you be in for a meal this evening, sir?'

And wondered why those dark grey eyes had widened as he simply stared at her for long moments, charged moments that set up a peculiar sensation deep in her tummy, robbing her of breath and turning her face brick-red before he muttered, 'No, Howard, I won't.'

*   *   *

Safely tucked away in the kitchen, Mercy gave up her attempts to eat her own toast and marmalade as her ears strained to hear the sound of his departure.

She so hoped she hadn't blown it. The legendary Andreo Pascali wouldn't stand for an underling telling him what to do. The trouble was that from the age of sixteen she had become used to running the household as she felt fit, looking after the family's slim budget, because her mother, poor darling, had gone to pieces after her husband's death and their consequent removal to the tiny cottage. And when she'd come up to London she'd swiftly been put in charge of her own team of cleaners so she'd grown used to deciding how and when things should be done. And maybe that wouldn't go down well with an Italian creative genius!

Yet she knew she was right. Her boss must work really hard to make such a success of his agency. He needed a decent breakfast. After all, he employed her to look after him, and that was what she would do.

The day flew by. Heartened by the growing conviction that she wasn't about to be made unemployed—an inspection of the breakfast tray informed her that Signor Pascali had eaten a slice of toast and one rasher of bacon, which meant that he hadn't taken her well-meaning lecture too badly—Mercy cleaned windows and polished furniture with gusto, making a mental note to ask him what his former housekeeper had done about ordering provisions and paying for them.

Apart from wine and coffee and a few ready meals languishing in the freezer, the cupboard was bare. She had had to pop out and buy the makings of today's spurned breakfast, and tomorrow's, out of her own slender resources. She'd thought her brother was undomesticated but her boss was in a league of his own!

At eight o'clock she called it a day. She was hot, grubby and smelled of floor polish and her feet ached. Popping a frozen meal in the microwave oven and assembling a tray, she promised herself a relaxing hour in front of the television in her own quarters, a hot bath and an early night. Grimacing because she knew Carly would say she'd been born middle-aged, she dropped what she was doing and hurried to answer the summons of the doorbell.

Signor Pascali? Forgotten his door key? She so wished she didn't look such a complete mess. No time to tidy herself up.

The opened door admitted a cooling river breeze and the blonde bombshell.

'I'm afraid he's out,' Mercy stated, breathing in an overpowering lungful of heady perfume.

'I know.' Trisha headed for the stairs. She was wearing a black dress that glittered as she moved. It clung to her magnificent bosom and voluptuous backside. 'He always stays late on a Tuesday. Brainstorming session, he calls it. I will wait for him in his bedroom. Be a good girl and bring a bottle of wine and two glasses.'

Despite her highly moral upbringing, Mercy wasn't a prude. People had 'partners' and 'relationships' instead of marriages. That didn't mean they didn't truly love each other. And a male as magnificent as Andreo would automatically choose a partner to match. So why did she sigh as she went to do as Trisha had asked?

Envy?

Utter nonsense!

'You didn't say whether you wanted red or white,' Mercy said brightly minutes later, entering Andreo's bedroom. 'So I brought both.'

The blonde was inspecting herself in the full length mirror, turning this way and that as if looking for reassurance. Glancing up after placing the bottles and glasses on the night table that flanked the bed—a heavily carved statement of opulence in the otherwise severely masculine room—Mercy noticed for the first time that the other woman was looking quite peaky underneath all that make-up, her full mouth trembling.

'Are you all right?'

'Just open the wine! No, the red,' she said as Mercy's hand reached for the white. 'I need some stiffening.' Sinking down on to the bed, she kicked off her high heels with edgy force and the hand that took the brimming glass was shaking.

Seeing the blonde sprawled out on the richly embroidered silk covers made Mercy's stomach roll over sickly but her intention to make a smart exit was stymied by a breathy, 'Keep me company for ten minutes?'

Regretting her by now cooling supper, because surely hunger pangs alone were responsible for the queasiness that had afflicted her on pairing the blonde with Andreo's bed, Mercy lowered herself down on the very edge of the mattress and asked bluntly, 'So what's wrong?' because something patently was.

Beautiful, self-assured women didn't seek the company of mere underlings unless they were troubled and couldn't bear being alone with their problems.

The glass swiftly emptied, Trisha swung her endless legs to the sage green carpet and gave herself a refill. Lifting her magnificent shoulders in a minimal shrug, she answered, 'Nothing that can't be sorted. I hope.'

As the 'I hope' bit had emerged on a decidedly wistful note, Mercy said bracingly, 'Think positive. Whenever I've had a problem—and, believe me, I've had a few—'

Uninterested in Mercy's problems, past or present, Trisha put in, 'You might as well know, it's common knowledge. Andreo and I—' her voice wobbled '—had a falling out. He was on the brink of asking me to marry him when it happened.' She slanted Mercy a sideways look. 'Do you know if he's seeing someone else? If some little harpie's got her claws into him?'

'I wouldn't know,' Mercy confessed, her ready sympathies aroused. She could understand any woman falling deeply in love with a stunner like the Italian legend and feeling utterly desolate if she thought she'd lost him. 'But if he's in love with you and was about to propose, then he's hardly likely to take up with someone else in a hurry, is he?' she soothed. 'It would have been a lovers' tiff, nothing serious. My friend Carly and her Darren were always having them. And they always kissed and made up. In fact they're soon to be married. So just hang on to what's positive—that you're both madly in love with each other.'

As her heartening speech had no effect other than earning herself a look of incredulous scorn, Mercy, wanting her supper and a well-earned spell of relaxation, got to her feet, adding a generous, 'You're so lovely, he's not going to risk losing you over some little disagreement.'

She had reached the door when Trisha said, visibly brightening, 'You're right, of course. So right! And, by the way, make yourself scarce, would you? His mood can be tricky after a Tuesday session. Don't want to make it worse, do we? No offence, but you're hardly a sight to make a man glad to be home, are you?'

Was that remark catty or what? Mercy fumed as she clumped down the stairs. Or had the other woman merely been stating the glaringly obvious?

Andreo paid the taxi off and sprinted over the paving blocks, his door key at the ready. At last he had it! The great idea—the idea that would make Coronet Ready Meals walk off the shelves.

Chewing over the new project after a hectic day's work, none of his team had been enthusiastic. Dreary and boring being the general consensus. Used to projects aimed at the wealthy and glamorous, something as mundane as frozen pies and peas in gloopy gravy was a challenge they didn't want to rise to. Who could make such dull stuff appear trendy or even remotely glossy, even if it was organic, low fat, low salt and boringly good for you?

'We're aiming at a different market,' he'd snapped. 'Forget the glitz. We've got to pitch good old plain wholesomeness—'

And then he'd had it—just like that! The earnest expression, the frumpy little personage telling him to eat his breakfast like a good little boy! All he had to do was persuade her, soft talk her if absolutely necessary. Of course he could hire a professional, set Make-up to work on her—fat suit, wig, that sort of stuff. But Howard was a natural. Just as she was.

Closing the door behind him, a clumping sound alerted him to the progress of the object of his thoughts descending the stairs. A slashing grin spread over his features as he watched her. Swamping overall, dumpy shape, manic hair, big shoes. Perfect!

Mercy faltered slightly then pressed on. He wasn't supposed to see her. According to Trisha she wasn't a sight that would make a man glad to be home, brighten his spirits. But he was in a good mood. He was leaning back against the door, his superb frame relaxed, the smile that made her feel all wobbly blindingly in evidence.

'Still working, Howard?' Should he broach the subject now? Perhaps not. She looked tired and not what he'd call receptive. The morning would be better.

There was a wealth of warm concern in those honey-eyed tones but Mercy ignored it. She wished he wouldn't call her by her surname. It made her feel completely sexless, light years away from the blonde sprawled out on that sinfully opulent bed, waiting for him.

'Just finishing, sir.' Mercy gathered her senses. What did it matter what he called her? As far as he was concerned she was sexless. An object hired to keep his home clean and his laundry under control. Then, discounting Trisha's final cutting remark because the woman was plainly upset and nervous, she descended the final steps and confided, 'Your girlfriend arrived a short while ago.' And, greatly daring, 'She's in your bedroom and very upset over your falling out,' and watched his dark eyes fill with outrage.

'Trisha?' Anger flamed in the look he trained on her.

'Of course.' Unable to keep the censure from her voice—how many girlfriends did he have?—she advised, 'It's no use getting cross. I don't know what caused the lovers' tiff and I don't want to, but you should talk it through calmly then kiss and make up. She's still the woman you wanted to marry and she's crazy about you and—'

'Just shut up!' Lean fingers fastened around her slender wrist. 'Upstairs. I need a witness.'

Hauled back upstairs at what felt like the speed of light, Mercy gasped, 'Have you gone crazy?' fell over her feet and gasped some more as a strong supporting arm whipped round her, forcing her on.

'No,' he gritted. 'Just furious! You will never let that woman into my home again, and that's an order.'

No reply was possible. The effect of being held against that lean hard body had taken her breath away, turned her legs to water and brought on that peculiar and rather shaming squirmy feeling deep inside her.

This was what being caught in a hurricane must feel like, Mercy decided wildly as she was abandoned just inside his bedroom door, staring at the inviting tableau on the bed. Trisha's big hair was artfully arranged against the pillows, the hem of her dress hiked indecently high. Her reaction when Andreo loomed over her was one of a purring kitten having its tummy tickled, turning to spitting fury as her sultry eyes landed on Mercy, who was still breathless and oddly shaky.

The hurricane had now been transformed into an iceberg. The chillingly sculpted features looked merciless as he used his mobile phone, his voice an arctic blast as he informed, 'A cab will be here in five minutes to take you home. I suggest you wait for it outside. The affair is dead, as you very well know. It could have ended amicably. You know the rules. As it is, if you try to contact me, come within a hundred yards, I shall slap a restraining order on you so fast you won't know what hit you.'

As the other woman headed for the door, her lovely face a mask of vindictive anger, Mercy plopped down on the linen press at the foot of the bed, not trusting her legs to hold her upright a moment longer. 'That was so cruel!' she gasped, her huge eyes wide with pained condemnation.

His frown pleating his brow, he turned glinting, incredulous pewter eyes on her as if, Mercy thought edgily, a speck of dust beneath his feet had suddenly flown up and bitten him on the nose. But she soldiered on regardless because she had never been able to abide injustice. 'The poor woman is plainly in love with you. She didn't deserve that sort of treatment.'

Bang went her job, she decided sickly as icy silence fell around her, making her skin prickle. Her castigation might have been excused had she been an old and valued retainer, looking after him since he'd been two days old.

She'd been with him two days and already she was lecturing him on his bad behaviour! Why couldn't she learn to keep her thoughts to herself? Her hands twisted nervously in her lap.

Santo cielo! How dared she call his actions into question, moralise, spout such nonsense? Andreo questioned with grim incredulity. Opening his mouth to tell her to get out of his sight and watch her tongue in future if she wanted to hang on to her cushy job, he reminded himself of the favour he wanted of her and smartly closed it again.

A woman of her strait-laced and probably sheltered background wouldn't have a clue, he told himself tersely, relaxing his shoulders. He wouldn't have involved her in this unpleasantness but he'd needed a witness in case he had to go for a restraining order.

'I'm sorry you think that,' he ground out. He never explained himself to anyone but now, in fairness, he supposed he had to bite the bullet. The righteous fire had left her eyes—stunning eyes, he noted with a stab of surprise—and she was now looking downtrodden and dejected.

Smothering a huff of impatience, he wheeled away. He had no reason to feel sorry for her. She was more than capable of standing up for herself. He'd been on the receiving end of more lectures in the short time she'd been working for him than he'd had to endure during the whole of his thirty-one years!

Pouring wine into the unused glass—clearly part of the kiss and make up scenario Trisha had had in mind—he handed it to her and said with a gentleness that further surprised him, 'Don't tell me that alcohol never passes your lips, Howard. It will help you recover from the unpleasant scene I forced you to witness.'

Stung, her fingers closed around the stem of the glass. What did he think she was? Some kind of hopelessly pious prude? Just because her father had been a man of the cloth!

'I do take the occasional drink, *signor*.' A barefaced lie. She had never been able to afford the stuff. 'And I don't wear a hair shirt, either!'

'*Touché!*' Andreo's sensual mouth quirked as he watched her drain the glass in two reckless gulps. 'And to put the record straight, I never had any intention of marrying Trisha Lomax—or tying myself down to any woman, come to that. She knew it. She knew exactly what to expect, I promise you. While the affair lasted—and it turned out to be of short duration—she would enjoy my complete fidelity, and when it was over there would be no hard feelings and a handsome gift as a token of my regard and respect.'

Wondering if she had the remotest idea of how these things worked, and further wondering why he should care, Andreo sat beside her on the press, prising the empty glass from her fingers and setting it on the floor, informing her drily, 'Such arrangements aren't unheard of.'

Mercy's head was swimming. This close to him she felt light-headed, hot and bothered all over. 'It sounds immoral to me,' she muttered. Her mouth felt numb and peculiar. She really should have fought the nervous tension that had led her to swallow all that wine like that. 'Have you thought that the poor woman might have fallen in love with you?' As any woman with eyes to see and a spark of life left in her body would.

Dio mio! Give me patience! Andreo stemmed the

impulse to tell her not to talk such juvenile rubbish. For the time being he needed her on side. 'A woman whose feelings were deeply engaged would have returned the suite of diamonds—the parting gift, remember?' he enforced through gritted teeth. 'Neither would she have hung on to the numerous costly trinkets she batted her eyes at during our time together. The only thing Trisha Lomax loved, apart from herself, was the size of my bank account, which goes a long way to explaining why she was misguided enough to believe she could change my mind about marriage.'

About to inform him that that was a highly selfish and jaundiced view, Mercy fell silent when he went on to tell her without a hint of self-pity, 'Since I reached my late teens women have been throwing themselves at me. As a testosterone-fired young man I thought I was in heaven until my grandfather, the wisest man I have ever known, warned me. The hearts that beat within those delightful breasts are full of avarice, he advised—from experience—pointing out that the size of the Pascali family fortune was well known. Enjoy the lovely creatures by all means, but never commit, he said to me. Marry when the need for an heir becomes paramount but choose a bride with wealth of her own, even if she has a face like a dustbin—glamorous mistresses are ten a penny.'

'I've shocked you,' Andreo commiserated, misconstruing his housekeeper's appalled expression. Springing to his feet, he paced across the room to refill her wineglass. 'But I wanted you to know where I'm coming from and to stop you accusing me of breaking that woman's heart. The only difference between her and the rest is that she didn't stick by the rules. She decided she could persuade me to marry her. As if!'

His brow suddenly clenching, Andreo vented an impatient sigh. He never explained himself, as he'd reminded himself once before this evening. So why break the habit of a lifetime now? Howard was his housekeeper, hired to iron his socks—or whatever was done to them—not to be privy to his lifestyle.

Handing her the glass, his brow cleared. Those amazingly big blue eyes were drenched with sympathy—maybe something could be done about them—mud-coloured contact lenses, perhaps?

Lowering himself beside her, he congratulated himself that at last she was on side. After what he'd told her she would be seeing through whatever sob story Trisha had come out with. No more righteous and misguided accusations of cruelty to make her prim her mouth and categorically refuse to do as he wanted.

Her heart swelling with pity and something else entirely as the devastating Italian again joined her on the press, Mercy stared at the glass in her hands. She hadn't asked for it and didn't want it—already her head was feeling peculiar. But she felt so achingly sorry for him she just couldn't bring herself to thrust it back at him. Poor, poor thing!

He was so gorgeous, so vital, how could he believe no woman could love him for himself and not his bank balance? She could throttle his cynical old grandfather for planting the idea in his head! He must feel so lonely!

'Howard…'

'Yes, sir?' Mercy glanced up at his low-pitched murmur then hurriedly transferred her gaze back to the glass she was holding. His eyes were a gleam of pure silver beneath the heavy dark fringe of his lashes and the long line of his mouth had softened with outrageous sensuality. Like a man looking at an object of desire.

Her cheeks blossoming with wild colour, she berated herself for thinking like a lunatic and buried her nose in her glass for something to do with herself just as he said, 'Cut out the "sirs". We're friends, right?'

He'd angled himself so that he was looking directly at her and here, in the intimacy of his bedroom, with him so close, close enough to smell the faint lemony drift of his aftershave, feel his body heat, it made her insides curl up with tension, her breath come in strange little gasps, her entire body tingle in a way she had never experienced before.

'Er—right,' she gulped strainedly and frantically tried to pull herself together. 'Friends' was okay. Normal, really. And with his track record he'd be used to looking at a woman—any woman from one-year-old to a hundred—that way. Just a habit. She was busy blaming her silliness on her unaccustomed intake of alcohol until he said, his dark velvet voice liberally smeared with honey, 'I have a proposition to put to you.'

CHAPTER THREE

'AND that is?' Mercy tried her best to sound bright and interested. Difficult when her tongue felt three feet thick. If this was what being tiddly was like she hated it. Cursing her foolishness in so innocently drinking that first glass as if it were as innocuous as fruit juice and then taking polite sips of the unwanted second, she did her best to concentrate on what he was saying.

'I want you to model for me.'

For a moment she could only gape at him. Had the alcohol affected her hearing too? Messed with her brain? Mercy's poleaxed eyes clung to his. Big mistake, she groaned inwardly. He was looking at her that way again, soft silver lights in those stunning eyes as they held her own confused gaze, his bewitching lips parted in a sensual half smile. She swallowed thickly and shook her head, trying to clear it of the muddle inside.

'What did you say?'

'That you'd be perfect for a project I'm currently working on.'

To her intense amazement and quivering delight his lean long-fingered hands softly cupped her face, lifting it to his openly assessing gaze. Mercy shook with inner tremors as her whole body seemed to catch fire, burn and shiver at the same time.

He looked as if he were about to kiss her, she

thought wildly as her veins pulsed with dangerous excitement. Unbidden, her soft mouth parted with yearning anticipation as his eyes roamed over every feature then slowly dropped to what he could see of her body—mainly and shamingly the way her regrettably generous breasts were pushing against the now rather grubby grey fabric of her overall.

'You'd have the small but absolutely pivotal role in the commercial we're about to film... Just a few hours of your time... Coronet... You'd be so perfect...'

There was a strange buzzing sound inside her head. Mercy simply couldn't process what he was saying. It all sounded so incredible she didn't have a clue to how she could begin to understand it. She only knew she deeply mourned the loss of the sizzling, paralysing effect of his cool skin against her burning cheeks when he dropped his hands and took the dangerously tilting wineglass from hers, then mentioned a payment that sounded so crazily huge she could only gulp in frantic disbelief.

'Think it over,' he advised, still employing the silky-soft seductive tone that made every muscle, bone and nerve-ending she possessed go into meltdown. Elevating his lean frame with effortless ease, he took her hands and drew her to her feet, her body brushing against his as she rose, making her need, quite desperately, to sit straight back down again because her legs had gone.

But he was crossing the floor, long energetic strides taking him to the door. Holding it open for her, he gave her the benefit of that totally charismatic smile.

'If you agree you'd be doing me a big favour. Sleep on it, and we'll iron out the details in the morning.'

Having to call on every scrap of will-power she possessed, Mercy managed to stay upright and relatively steady as she left the room and headed for her bed, all thoughts of supper and the hot bath she'd promised herself abandoned in the pressing need to seek oblivion. All the while she shakily promised herself that she'd figure out exactly what had happened in his room this evening when her brain wasn't in shock and fuddled with alcohol.

'Oh, wow!' Carly screeched.

Mercy snatched the mobile phone off her ear and shifted in one of the comfy armchairs in her private sitting room, only returning to the conversation when she judged she was in no further danger of having her eardrum split.

'I didn't take it in properly last evening—' she came clean '—I'd had the best part of two huge glasses of wine and—'

'You never!' Carly groaned theatrically. 'You know it goes straight to your head! Remember that Christmas when you got squiffy on one spoonful of rum sauce!'

'Well, the wine was given to me with all good intentions and it seemed rude not to drink it,' Mercy excused lamely then went on to recount what she'd thought had been said, editing out her crass stupidity in thinking for one moment that he had been about to kiss her. As if!

'But he cleared it up this morning when I took him his breakfast.' A warm smile lit her features. He'd looked really pained at first but he'd eaten every scrap of the kedgeree after she'd told him, very firmly—no messing—that fish was good brain food. 'I'm to go to the studio next Monday and present myself to Make-up and Wardrobe. They'll start filming my part some time after midday, depending on how the location shots go, apparently. And he's paying mega bucks so I'll really be able to make a huge difference for James. He can forget about taking out further student loans in the forseeable future.'

Carly heaved a sigh. 'I don't believe this!'

'No, neither do I,' Mercy confided. 'How anyone could think I'd be a perfect model for a TV ad—'

'I mean I don't believe you wouldn't want to spend at least some of all that dosh on nice things for yourself,' the other woman corrected tartly. 'For as long as I've known you, you've always put yourself and what you wanted last on your list of priorities! But I guess nagging won't change you.' Her tone lightened. 'And I do believe you'd make great model material. Your brilliant boss must have taken one look at you and seen the potential. Haven't I always told you you could be drop-dead-gorgeous if you took trouble with your appearance? Stopped buying the dreary stuff you call essentials from charity shops, had your hair done properly and let me do your make-up. He obviously looked at you and saw star material!' she enthused as Mercy struggled not to hoot out loud at that unlikely scenario. 'And how about inviting me over one evening? I bet his pad's fabulous—I'm dying to see inside! And what will your ad be plugging?'

'I'm not sure,' Mercy confessed, feeling foolish. 'He mentioned something about Coronet and some-

thing or other last night. And I didn't like to ask him
to repeat himself this morning. He would only have
thought I hadn't been listening to a word he'd said.'
Which she hadn't. Only she couldn't, for shame, further confess that she'd been too busy wondering if he
was about to kiss her and coming over all silly and
unnecessary!

'Coronet,' Carly mused. 'I'd have heard, surely, if
there was a new ultra-expensive brand of perfume or
make-up about to hit the market. Whatever, it's bound
to be something eye-wateringly glamorous! Jewellery,
perhaps? His agency's famous for handling the top
end of the glitz market—they don't touch dreary stuff
like washing powder and loo cleaners!'

After listening to a lot more on the same lines—
like her face would become a national byword for all
that was glamorous and sophisticated, not to mention
her fortune—and promising to ask Andreo if she had
his permission to invite Carly over one evening,
Mercy ended the call, curled up more comfortably
and wallowed in what her friend had said.

Could it really be possible that the super-
charismatic, utterly gorgeous Italian legend had seen
something that her mirror had staunchly withheld
from her? That he had looked at her with desire? That
he had been about to kiss her but had held back, afraid
such an action might spoil their working relationship?
The idea sent delicious tremors zipping down her
spine.

Then, coming to her senses, obliterating the schoolgirl fantasies, which up until now she had never been
prey to, she posed another question.

Could pigs fly?

In any case, she wouldn't want him to kiss her, would she? she told herself firmly, regaining her fabled common sense. No doubt he'd be very good at it, whirling a girl off to paradise with practised ease. But what girl with any self-respect and half a brain in her head would want to be romanced by a man with the morals of a feral tom-cat and the attention span of a toddler where the females in his life were concerned?

Sitting in front of a huge mirror, dazzled by lights that were shining straight into her face, Mercy could hardly contain her excitement or the nerves that were making her bloodstream fizz and her stomach lurch.

Having delivered her, Andreo had disappeared, and Make-up and Wardrobe were in a huddle in the doorway. Several utterly lovely scantily-clad females and one blond male model type had wandered through during the time she'd been left here to stew. And wonder. If she knew what she was supposed to say and do...

Smartly switching that thought off because it only served to make her even more nervous and more convinced than ever that she couldn't act to save her life and would be thrown off the set and lose the fat fee that would be such a help to James, she turned her mind to calmer thoughts.

Since she'd agreed to do as he'd asked, her boss had been sweetness and light, coming home for supper every evening, inviting her to join him and entrancing her with the dry humour that made for effortless conversation. He hadn't even shown the slightest irritation with her unclued-up state when she'd broached the subject of housekeeping money, merely giving her that toe-curling smile and explaining, 'Knox ordered whatever was needed from Harrods. All you have to do is pick the phone up, take delivery and leave me to pay the bills.'

'Such profligacy!' she'd scolded, quite unable to help herself. 'I could shop much more cheaply. I have plenty of time to spare to head for the markets and find bargains! Have you never heard the saying—look after the pennies and the pounds will look after themselves?'

He'd thrown back his handsome head and roared with laughter, covering her with confusion and making her blush to the roots of her hair as she considered the fact that the super-wealthy would never need to bother themselves with penny-pinching trifles. In future she'd keep her mouth zipped on the subject of economy drives.

They'd rubbed along remarkably well, considering, she reflected. And she'd got over her silliness. Of course she thought he was an absolute dish—what woman wouldn't? And she could be excused for being unable to take her eyes off him, couldn't she? He was so exotic. Like a peacock in a flock of grey geese. So of course she would find him utterly fascinating; she wouldn't be human if she didn't. That didn't mean she was interested in him in a man/woman way. As if!

No, the right man for her would be steady and reliable, faithful, good husband and father material, and it wouldn't matter a toss what he looked like or how much money he had stashed away in the bank!

And if sometimes she wandered off into a daydream that featured her—transformed into a thing of beauty, courtesy of the two young women she'd been handed over to and clever studio lighting—and her boss seeing her as a desirable female instead of boring old Howard, then she couldn't exactly blame herself, not when the magical, eagerly awaited transformation would shortly take place.

'This is for you.' A thin young man floated past, pushing a sheaf of papers into her hands. Jerked out of her calming reverie, Mercy gathered it was her script or something. The typed heading read Coronet RMs.

Rapidly scanning, hoping she didn't have too many lines to learn, Mercy's blood ran cold then soared up to boiling point.

She didn't have to say a word.

She just had to stand around looking frumpy while the handsome male model ignored the wiles of a bevy of lovely young things, the enticement of smart restaurants, jumped in his Ferrari and drove at speed to where she, the ugly, frumpy one was serving up a Coronet Ready Meal, earning herself an adoring look of devotion!

Mercy felt sick and then furious. That was how Andreo Pascali saw her! Boring, frumpy and downright ugly!

She hated him!

How could she have been so vain as to be flattered when he'd all but begged her to feature in his rotten commercial? More than half believing Carly when she'd gushed about him seeing her potential! Indulging in ridiculous daydreams that had embarrassed her just as much as they had excited her!

She hated herself!

No wonder she'd been left to stew while the beautiful things were filming on location. On the point of storming out, leaving Andreo Pascali to search for someone as ugly as she was, she subsided with gritted teeth. Whatever her personal feelings—and they were murderous!—she couldn't pass up the opportunity to really help James financially.

'Sorry you've been kept waiting.' The perky young thing from Make-up smiled at her reflection in the mirror. 'Would you like a coffee or something?'

Not trusting herself to utter a word that didn't come out on a savage hiss, Mercy shook her head. She couldn't swallow a thing, even though she'd broken her cardinal rule and skipped breakfast in the excitement of getting ready to accompany an over-solicitous Andreo to the studio.

Rat!

'Then we'll get to work.'

'Won't have to do much,' Mercy mumbled, rage suddenly subsiding, leaving an unwelcome feeling of desperate hurt in the region of her heart.

'Don't you believe it!' was the chirpy response. 'I'm Trixie, by the way.' She picked up a handful of wild toffee-coloured curls. 'Your hair's such a lovely colour and in glorious condition.' A fistful of gunk was produced. 'This will dull it down and flatten it— don't worry, it'll wash out. Remember,' Trixie soothed as the flattened hair was pulled into a knot at her nape, 'the theme of the ad is the way to a man's heart and so on. In spite of the temptations on offer, the guy only has eyes for his stodgy, wholesome, caring wife! Especially when he knows he can come home to a Coronet meal.'

Hysteria threatening, Mercy choked on a peal of manic laughter and submitted to having beige-toned foundation smoothed on to her face and dark-framed plain-lensed glasses perched on her nose. Wardrobe fastened something resembling a bolster around her hips before dressing her in a beige-coloured sack-like dress.

So much for the glamour of fabulous jewellery or wildly expensive sports cars with her clothed in something tastefully sexy, magically transformed into a knock-'em-dead beauty with Andreo looking on proudly, saying, 'By Jove, she's got it!' or something along those lines and feeling all possessive of the wonderful creature he'd created!

This humiliation served her right for allowing herself, in those quiet moments when her brain and heart forgot to be sensible, to harbour such absurdities!

The third take had been perfect. Andreo rose from his seat beyond the studio lights. The first two had been disasters, wooden, with Howard looking bad-tempered—as if she'd wanted to push the steaming dish of what he'd been told was halibut and broccoli in some sauce or other right into someone's face.

His, judging by the scowl she'd shot in his direction. 'Smile,' he'd instructed on a snap. 'You are presenting your husband with a delicious, wholesome meal—not asking him why he forgot to fix the drains, woman!'

Thankfully, she'd taken his coming-to-the-end-of-his-tether instruction on board. Remembering the fat fee, he guessed, as she'd done as he'd demanded. She had a truly beautiful smile, he noted, not for the first time. Like sunshine, he congratulated himself. Warm, caring, beneficent. Without a trace of artifice. Wholesome. Just what he'd known would tie in perfectly with the product. Underlining the story-line— a real man went for plain wholesome goodness rather than sophisticated, superficial sexy glitter.

'I'll pick you up in half an hour,' he told her as he walked her back to Make-up. Why wasn't she chattering as she usually did? he wondered. Or gazing up at him with those wide, deep blue eyes? Walking stiffly, her neat profile presented to him, she looked drained. Could be down to the sludgy make-up that covered her set features.

Or the heat of the lights. He had to remember she wasn't a professional. It had probably been a pretty fraught experience for her—especially when he'd lost his always precarious patience and yelled at her.

'You were perfect,' he told her as he ushered her through the door. Plainly she needed reassurance. 'Well done, Howard!'

He turned to return to the camera crew, dismissing her from his agile mind.

Soft-soaping rat! Mercy fulminated as she submitted to having her face cleansed and the gunk washed out of her hair, taking her anger out on him as a change from castigating herself for fantasising about him doing a Pygmalion act and transforming her into something she never could be.

Dressed in her boxy grey suit, her hair again a mass of writhing corkscrew curls, her face pink with recent humiliation, Mercy was ready when he breezed through the door, all confident alpha male in his impeccable suit and hand-stitched shoes, the charismatic focus of Trixie's avid gaze.

Mercy didn't look at him. She wanted no reminders of the yawning gulf between her and this example of Italian male perfection.

Get over it! she grumped at herself as Andreo imperiously hailed a taxi and handed her in. So she'd indulged in a secret fantasy, left her wits behind her from time to time. No big deal. Show her the plain female who hadn't briefly yearned for an out of reach, superb specimen of virile masculinity and she'd produce a unicorn out of a conjurer's hat! From now on, fantasies were definitely out!

Ten minutes later, finding herself outside a classy-looking restaurant as Andreo paid off the taxi, Mercy frowned. Her 'What are we doing here?' came out sounding like an accusation as she forced herself to look up at him.

'We are about to eat.' His firm hand cupped her elbow. 'You've had a tiring day, Howard. Feeding you, instead of expecting you to slave over a hot stove to feed me, is my way of thanking you personally for today.'

'There's no need,' Mercy objected, rooting her feet in their sensible lace-ups to the pavement. 'You pay me to make your meals.' And if that sounded ungracious, she didn't care. 'I'm not dressed to dine anywhere smart!' she blurted. She was not in the mood to share a table with a man who saw her as an obliging frumpy lump, was her agonised thought.

'Don't be silly, Howard.' That fascinating mouth formed a straight line of authority. The pressure of his hand increased as he drew her forward. 'You look fine. No one will look at you, in any case.'

And they didn't. Heads turned as Andreo strode confidently into the rarefied atmosphere. Expertly styled female heads on top of beautifully dressed svelte bodies, heads with openly admiring eyes, following his progress to an inner table.

Mercy shuddered. She felt like an elephant lumbering through a herd of ultra-refined gazelles as Andreo guided her forward, one hand firmly on the small of her back. And when her bulky handbag thumped against a black-clad shoulder, sending the poor man's loaded fork flying out of his hand and she trod on it she wished she could disappear in a puff of smoke and never be seen again. She couldn't stop apologising volubly until Andreo beckoned a waiter, added his own softly voiced apology and urged Mercy towards their table.

Subsiding into the seat the waiter held out for her, her face flaming, Mercy couldn't speak for hating her boss for his poise, for the way the fine expensive fabric of his suit jacket skimmed his wide shoulders with impeccable ease, for the sleek narrowness of his waistline and hips and the length of his narrow-trousered legs. Hated him for his insistence they eat here, hated him for being so gorgeous!

As he took his seat opposite, the waiter handed her a menu the size of a broadsheet and her instinct was to hide behind it. But she didn't.

She dropped it on the table and glared ahead, past the menu Andreo was consulting. She noted the way a perfectly groomed blonde was staring at her, then looking quickly away, saying something to her companion who grinned broadly, lobbed her, Mercy, a quick glance and said something that made the blonde trill with laughter.

Knowing her face had turned the colour of pickled beetroot made Mercy feel a thousand times worse. If she'd thought she could make a dignified departure without knocking people's food out of their mouths she would have walked out. As it was, Andreo lowered his menu, noted her mutinous expression and ordered for both of them.

Alone, or as alone as they could be in a roomful of beautiful chattering people, Mercy could contain her feelings no longer.

'Take me home!'

'Why?' Andreo regarded his housekeeper steadily, doing his utmost not to grin. Her face was red. Too hot in that unbecoming jacket? Her jaw was pugnacious, her lips grimly clamped together. If any other female had made that bitten-out request he would have complied immediately, escorted her home with cool, taut dignity and written her off, consigning her to limbo without a thought.

But Howard amused him and that was an absolute first. Knox had been dour, speaking only when spoken to and, to a woman, the sexy females who had briefly shared his spare time had been cloying, provoking, in the end, boredom. No one could accuse Howard of being sexy but her unconscious ability to amuse him made him want to humour her. 'Don't you like it here?' He used his lightest, most cajoling tone, leaning forward a little, his eyes searching her set-rigid features, suddenly, puzzlingly, wanting to see that beautiful smile.

It didn't materialise. But a hissed explosion of anger did. 'Do you go out of your way to humiliate me? Or does hurting people's feelings just come naturally?'

She watched his face go still. Very still. His eyes intent on hers, he asked softly, with a thread of venom, 'What do you mean?'

The realisation that she'd probably just got herself the sack because no one, but no one, could get away with criticising Andreo Pascali and hope to avoid due punishment did nothing to stop her. She was beyond caring. 'This—' An arm waved widely, coming within a whisker of toppling the stem vase holding a single red rose on the table between them. 'This place. With me looking like—like me! And people laughing at me. And you wanting me to wave a plate of food around in a commercial because I'm what you wanted. Ugly! And boring!' Her eyes brimmed with despised moisture. Feeble! But she was sure everyone in this horrible restaurant would have heard every spitting, hissing word and that was an added humiliation.

'Don't!' Appalled, Andreo reached across the table and took one hand, gently unfisting the fingers. He noted the way her big, angry, glittering eyes widened at his touch, the way she drew in a ragged breath as if to stop whatever she'd been about to come out with next. Poor old Howard! The thought of hurting her— even though he hadn't meant to—was distressing.

Strange, that. His brows clenched in amazement. He rarely gave a thought to other people's feelings. He had never had to. What he said went. Like gospel. 'You're not in the least ugly!' A seductive smile ousted the frown. Plain maybe, dumpy certainly, and no dress sense whatsoever. 'Not ugly,' he repeated, 'and certainly not boring,' winning the battle as he had been sure he would. Her shoulders were relaxing, the amazingly blue eyes melting, no longer shooting daggers into his soul! 'I saw you as a wholesome, caring woman presenting her husband with his favourite meal. The sort of homey soul a real man would prefer over any number of selfish me-me-me bimbos!'

Well, it was part of the truth, he excused himself blithely. It would be counter-productive to explain his true thinking: that any man would be putty in the hands of the plainest woman if she routinely dished up the product. Unmollified, she was likely to sweep out, knocking plates, food, cutlery, glasses off tables with that bloated bag thing!

Seizing the advantage of her limpid silence, the way her mouth was silenced, softening from that grim line, he gave her hand a final squeeze before relinquishing it and telling her in all truthfulness, 'I brought you here to save you the bother of having to cook after your wonderful performance this afternoon. And because the food's excellent. And I don't mind that you're wearing your everyday clothes while everyone else is dressed up to the nines. And if I don't mind—' he gave her his ravishing smile '—I don't see why you should.'

CHAPTER FOUR

LOOKING back over that evening, only one thing still rankled. Oh, the food had been delicious, the appetite she'd thought she'd lost for the duration coming back with a vengeance. She'd even managed half a glass of the champagne he'd ordered without doing, saying or thinking anything too ridiculous.

She hadn't meant to cuddle his satisfyingly vehement denial of her ugliness to her like a comfort blanket, but she had. And had accepted his explanation of how he'd seen her in the food commercial at face value and positively glowed when she remembered him saying that a real man would choose a wholesome, caring woman over a superficial me-me-me bimbo!

It had been soothing ointment on the raw wound of her humiliation but now, almost a fortnight later, something he'd said still rankled.

But what?

She hadn't had time to really think hard about what was still annoyingly bugging her, something he'd said or implied that she was failing to access, because since the day of the shoot he'd been back to his truly unpredictable self. Sometimes he'd whisked himself off the moment he'd swallowed his breakfast and had not returned until the small hours, but more often he stayed home, shut in his office, banging away frantically on his keyboard, alternately yelling or purring down the telephone, bellowing for her to bring more coffee, empty his wastepaper basket, turn the central heating off, then turn it on again!

Entertaining an important client and his wife for dinner one evening, he had given her a truly tough time when he'd discovered, moments before the arrival of his guests, that instead of using his usual caterers she'd produced the meal herself at a fraction of the price, hotly accusing her of bourgeois penny-pinching, threatening her with dire punishment if the meal fell a fraction short of perfection. He had then disarmed her utterly when, his guests gone, he'd run her to earth in the kitchen, tidying up and grumbling to herself about ungrateful wretches, enfolding her in a bear hug and crowing, 'Congratulations, Howard! No one could have produced a better meal! Am I forgiven?'

Could anyone wonder that her head was in a permanent spin?

Today the luxury of complete silence was hers, but somehow, instead of feeling nice and relaxed because she wouldn't have to second guess what his volatile nature would demand of her next, she felt strangely empty. At six this morning he'd left for his flight to Rome. Business. He'd be away a week, maybe longer, so she could take it easy, do whatever she did in her time off.

'Where's my damn bag, Howard?' he'd demanded as he'd loped down the stairs.

She'd used the bright, no nonsense tone she employed when he looked like being difficult and pointed to the hide suitcase she'd packed for him the day before. 'Right there, sir. Your taxi's waiting.'

Suddenly pausing in his headlong dash across the vast hallway, he'd shot at her, 'And what do you do in your spare time, Howard?' Sounding as if he didn't trust her to behave herself. 'And don't call me sir.'

What did he think she did? she had thought crossly. Throw wild parties, go to raves? Go and mug old ladies outside post offices? Resisting the impulse to tell him to mind his own business, she contented herself with, 'The driver's already been waiting for five minutes,' crossing to open the door for him. 'Now, are you quite sure you have all your travel documents?'

The look he had given her would have withered a full grown oak in all its majesty. 'I am not a child, Howard. And you are not my nanny!' before grabbing his case and stalking out, very much on his impressive dignity.

Mercy sighed. He was impossible! But she wouldn't have him any other way. Never a dull moment and utterly gorgeous with it, she thought as she reached for her mid-morning coffee, feeling her eyelids droop. He'd kept her up late the night before, helping him to find the papers he needed for the Rome trip amidst the disorganised heap on his desk, not to mention every other work surface in his office, and then hunting down an elusive briefcase, grumping at her to use her eyes and her grumping right back, telling him that if he allowed her to tidy his office—which he categorically didn't—it might not be such an almighty shambles.

A soft smile curved her lips. Since working for the great Andreo Pascali she had never felt so alive; countering every emotion he put her through, be it anger, humiliation, amusement when he shared a joke with her, the sheer joy of those suppers he insisted they share, certainly kept her on her toes.

He was so vital, so mercurial, she never knew when those silvery eyes would darken with anger or glint with laughter or shimmer with the all-enveloping charm he could summon at will—usually, in her case, when he'd said or done something to make her seethe!

No wonder he could turn any woman he momentarily fancied into a sex slave, resistance impossible, poor things.

Thankfully, she would never number amongst his effortless conquests, she would never have to face the acid test of having to resist him. To him she was just plain old Howard, on hand to minister to his household needs, take the brunt of his temper tantrums because she was being paid handsomely to put up with them, enjoy the pleasant times, the periods of calm water when he treated her like a best mate.

Draining her coffee cup, she put it down with a clatter that threatened to break the saucer. That was it! The niggle at the back of her mind. 'I don't care what you look like, so why should you?'

But she did care and for the first time in her life she actually admitted it to herself. Strictly brought up by parents who were at pains to impress the selfishness of spending unnecessary money on oneself when there were millions in the world dying of starvation, lack of shelter and preventable diseases, her overactive conscience had always given her a mental flaying on the rare occasions when she'd drooled over some out-of-her-reach outfit in a classy shop window.

Any spare money had always been donated to a worthwhile charity, but after her father's death there had been precious little to spare and what had been scraped together by painful economies had been put aside for her clever brother's education.

But things were different now, weren't they? And she didn't want to make the most of herself for her boss's sake. Definitely not! He didn't give a toss what she looked like.

Dialling Carly's number, she hoped her friend wasn't having a longer than usual Sunday morning lie-in.

She had offered her help on several occasions. Mercy needed that help right now!

Mercy couldn't get enough of the image of her new self reflected in the full-length mirror in her bathroom. Last Sunday Carly had promised to book a day off on the following Friday, the day her colleague was due back from leave, sounding excited at the prospect. But as the week had progressed Mercy had had misgivings, strong ones—to the point of phoning her friend to cancel the whole thing. Her father would have sternly berated her for her vanity and her mother would have had a fit at what she would call a waste of good money.

But, 'I refuse to let you chicken out now!' Carly had yelled at her. 'Do you have any idea what a job I had to get Friday off? It's one of our busiest days. I had to practically go down on my knees and beg Sandra to say she could cope—I've covered for her often enough—so your transformation's on or I'll never speak to you again! Besides, you owe it to yourself!'

Capitulating, Mercy had reluctantly agreed that she did. With her vastly increased salary, not to mention the fat fee from modelling for that hateful commercial, she could afford to spend something on herself for a change without depriving James.

And it had been so worth it! The top stylist's bill had shaken her rigid. But he'd worked miracles. Expertly layered, the unruly corkscrews had been replaced by feathery waves that softly brushed her forehead and gently curved against her neck. A neck spectacularly lengthened by the deep V of the sapphire silk sweater that clung to her generous breasts and gently skimmed her tiny waist, ending just short of the hipline of the knee-length narrow navy skirt; kitten heels completed the picture of businesslike femininity. There were other tops to team with this skirt and the spare fawn one, similarly narrow but slightly shorter.

Unsure of the way both skirts failed to disguise the hips and backside she viewed as unfashionably curvy, she'd been reaching for one of the fawn fully gathered numbers she'd spied on the rail when her friend had hissed, 'No you don't—if you've got it, flaunt it!'

For off-duty time Carly had talked her into splurging out on a wickedly expensive primrose-coloured linen suit, then allowed her to assuage her guilty feelings by picking out cheap cotton leggings with toning tops before dangling under her nose a fabulous silky cotton shift splashed all over with tawny flowers which she had been quite unable to resist.

Excitedly, she scrambled out of her new work day

clothes, not mourning the hideous grey overalls, and into her favourite. The shift dress.

The colours really suited her and the fit, the feel of the soft fabric against her skin made her feel more like a woman than she'd ever done before.

Amazing! The big blue eyes of her reflection sparkled back at her. Somehow, her features seemed more defined. All down to the make-up Carly had chosen for her and shown her how to use. A creamy foundation, a hint of blusher, misty eyeshadow—just a touch, and rose pink lipstick.

Wondering what the men in her life would think of her new, more feminine appearance, she decided that James wouldn't even notice any difference. From long experience she knew he rarely noticed anything going on around him, being too wrapped up in his own little academic world.

And, as for Andreo, well—a revealing squirm deep in her tummy warned her to switch that thought off pronto. Apart from being her employer, he wasn't in her life, she impressed upon herself, and any sneaky, wayward thoughts in the other direction had to be killed at birth!

Changing her shoes for the higher heels that went with this dress, she made a few tottery experimental turns around the room. Unused to anything other than sensible lace-ups, she knew she would have to get some practice in before she could walk in three inch heels with anything approaching confidence and headed, gingerly, for the gallery that ran round the conversion, linking the first and second storey bedrooms and the massive main staircase.

Finally getting the hang of it, she faced the head

of the stairs and took in a deep breath. If she could negotiate them without falling from top to bottom she would count herself well on the way to becoming an expert.

Thanking heaven that she had the place to herself for her no doubt ludicrous attempts to emulate a cat-walk model—Andreo was not expected back for another two days, and maybe not even then—Mercy laid her hand lightly on the polished handrail and began to descend.

Andreo slotted the key into the main door. His pitch had been successful—he had never doubted it would be—and he had secured a highly lucrative deal, one that would only add further kudos to his agency's reputation. Normally he would have stayed on in the Rome apartment for a day or two, unwinding and enjoying the beautiful city, but for some reason he had headed straight back to London.

Dumping his suitcase just inside the door—Howard could deal with it, give her something to do after her near week of idleness—he found himself wondering what she had done with all that spare time. Taken a crash course on How To Be Even More Bossy, he conjectured with a grin.

Opening his mouth to shout her name, alert her to his return and demand a drink and something to eat that wasn't made up of airline plastic, he shut it again as he glimpsed a pale movement in the shadows at the head of the first flight of stairs.

Reaching sideways, he flicked on the overhead chandelier and light flooded the shadows, revealing a stranger.

A ravishing stranger.

His first thought was that Howard was entertaining friends, his second was *Madre di Dio*—Howard!

Howard, without those swamping overalls and that heavy, shapeless suit she seemed so attached to was sensational. Lush curves and a waist so tiny he could span it with his hands—who would have believed it!

Luscious!

If she hadn't been in his employ he would have been interested. Very interested! Marvelling that a frumpy lump could have been transformed into such a fabulous creature kept him dazed and speechless for the first time in his life and he only snapped himself together with an effort when her frozen stance was translated into flight.

'I need a drink, Howard.' His voice emerged on a roughened undertone. Raising it slightly, he issued, 'And something to eat. I'll join you in the kitchen. Ten minutes,' and tore his dazed eyes away, heading for his office to cool down. His libido seemed to be working overtime.

He needed every one of those ten minutes to haul himself together, convince himself that being turned on by his housekeeper was pathetic and ridiculous and he had never been either. Howard wearing a classy, understatedly sexy dress was still Howard. Still as bossy, ordering him around like a nanny in charge of a wilful child, answering back when he tore her off a strip. Still amusing when she took it into her head to lecture him about his hectic lifestyle and what she saw as his profligacy.

Endearingly amusing.

Heart hammering, Mercy made it to the kitchen. His totally unexpected early arrival had made her feel as if she were where she shouldn't be, doing something shameful. Horribly embarrassed.

Seeing him, staring down into that lean and darkly handsome face, had made her feel as if it was wicked to be so glad to see him, acknowledge how much she'd missed the impossible, infuriating, fascinating specimen of prime Italian masculinity. And the way he'd looked at her, those sleepily half-hooded eyes taking in every detail from the top of her newly styled hair, lingering on the swell of breasts, which she knew to her utter shame were standing to attention, then on and down to the suddenly shaky legs revealed by the above knee-length dress, had mesmerised her.

It had done her head in! And sent a *frisson* of electrifying sensation through her entire body, centring on the most private part of her. Mortification had arrowed through her at last and she'd been turning, intent on hiding herself from the lazily probing eyes that were making her feel all sorts of things she had no right feeling, when his rather huskily delivered order for sustenance had bumped her back into a shaky semblance of reality.

Her usual bustling efficiency having deserted her, Mercy stood in the large immaculate kitchen and dithered, staring into space, her mind stubbornly preoccupied with the way he'd been looking at her, making her feel strangely breathless until, the stark knowledge that the ten minutes he'd stipulated was now probably a mere five galvanised her into kicking off the impractical shoes, covering her finery with one of the big dreary overalls and diving for the fridge.

Thankfully, but tenuously, back into housekeeper mode she opened a bottle of the red wine he preferred, hurriedly threw together a green salad and was at the stove, pink-faced, heart bumping, when he said from right behind her, 'That smells good.'

'Just a simple herb omelette—' She bit back the 'sir' she trotted out when she wanted to underline that theirs was a formal employer/employee relationship. She didn't want to antagonise him—which would inevitably draw a lippy response from her. Sparks flying between them wouldn't be a good idea.

'Share it with me.'

No answer. A smile warmed his eyes as they approved the way her hair softly curved in fascinating little toffee-coloured tendrils against the creamy skin of her narrow nape.

'And that's an order.'

Hunting through cupboards, he located a second wineglass and rifled drawers for another set of cutlery. 'See how domesticated I can be!' he remarked with what Mercy considered to be male puffed-up pride, totally unwarranted because he was as domesticated as a wild tiger.

So that ridiculous remark deserved no response, she decided as she approached with the omelette, proud of her serene housekeeperly outward appearance when inside she was still hot and squirmy over what she had seen in his eyes as he'd so slowly absorbed her newly transformed self.

'So where's yours?' Andreo looked up from the mouth-watering golden fluffy offering she had slid in front of him to find her standing stiffly to attention,

her lush lips pressed together, those beautiful eyes
blank and distant.

'I've already eaten.' As good an excuse as any to
pass on a cosy supper for two. She needed to find her
shoes, get out of here and shut herself up with a lecture on the subject of abject foolishness. Andreo
Pascali, self-confessed womaniser, would look at any
half-way passable female in that—that lascivious
way!

'Then sit and talk to me. Help yourself to wine.'
His eyes promised severe retribution if she failed to
comply, Mercy recognised, totally used to the massive self assurance that demanded that he always got
his own way. A self-assurance that could only be
countered by one huge tussle. Mercy wasn't up to
tussle, not right now.

Ungraciously, she sat, reached for the bottle, filled
up his glass and gave herself a bare half an inch. She
definitely needed to keep a clear head; she no way
wanted to relax and enjoy his company, not while she
was still fizzing inside, feeling shaky and quite peculiar.

Helping himself to salad, Andreo stabbed out,
'Aren't you going to ask how the Rome trip went?'
It was not like Howard to behave like a stuffed
dummy. It was beginning to irritate him.

'I'm sure it went the way you wanted it to.' The
right repressive nanny-like tone, Mercy congratulated
herself and watched his spectacular eyes narrow and
wished she could stop herself wondering what it
would feel like to be kissed by him.

Andreo frowned. Laid down his fork. What had got
into her? He'd grown used to her lecturing, her

whacky ideas, her ready laughter when something amused her, her fussing and bustle. And then the light dawned. Of course!

Like any woman, Howard was miffed because the slightest alteration in her appearance hadn't been commented on and complimented. And in Howard's case the alteration had been spectacular. She was superb—monumentally lustworthy. Though he wouldn't dream of confiding that much. She was his employee. Out of bounds.

'You've had some of that mass of hair cut off,' he remarked, to show her he had noticed the result. The sexy result. Though that description was best kept to himself. 'Suits you.' And reapplied himself to the best omelette he had ever tasted, fully expecting that sop to her vanity to have done the trick.

It hadn't. Fingering the bowl of his wineglass, he frowned. She still looked stiff and buttoned up—and why had she spoiled the effect of the sleek dress that had shown her fantastic curves to full advantage with that swamping grey thing? Because the full impact of her delectable charms wasn't meant for his eyes? Whose eyes, then?

'You were on your way out to meet someone?' Some guy. Dressed like that, it had to be. And the question had come out like an accusation. Like a father addressing a wayward daughter!

'Use the phone and cancel!' he rapped out. Something hard and hot ricocheted through him, ending up in a knot in his chest. The thought of her being out on a date, coming home in the early hours, being pawed by some guy in the back of a taxi, made him feel nauseated. Filled him with a deep, black anger.

Because... Because—his fingers drummed against the table—because looking the way she did when she wasn't in her drab housekeeperly disguise meant that some guy would snap her up, whisk her away, and then where would he be? Wasting his time looking for another housekeeper to take her place. That was where!

Greatly relieved at having hit on the logical reason for his reaction, his hands relaxed, reaching again for his glass, his huskily accented voice smooth as cream as he glossed over the snapped out order that she cancel whatever on-the-town high-jinks she'd rigged herself up for. 'You've had the best part of a week to do your own thing, Howard. But I'm back now and naturally expect everything to roll along as smoothly as before.'

Meaning? Mercy stiffened. That she be on hand at all times, waiting, breath bated, for him to demand something, tell her what to do. And what not to do! Like go out on some evenings to enjoy herself, like other normal young women! Sometimes she wanted to hit him—she really did!

Bottling up the torrent of emotions that threatened to gush out and smother him with scorn, she pushed back her chair and informed him with what she hoped was dignity, 'There is nothing to cancel. And if there's nothing more you require, I'll say goodnight.' Not looking at him, she swept to the door, gathering her shoes on the way, pausing for a fraction in the doorway to end with a defiant, 'Sir!'

CHAPTER FIVE

'DON'T even think it!' Mercy said tartly, bending over to place the bowl of mueseli—hamster litter, as named by Andreo Pascali—and wholemeal toast in front of him. 'It's good for you.'

Andreo felt a violent inner shudder rake up from the soles of his expensively shod feet. Nothing to do with the breakfast she'd served up this morning. He was actually developing a taste for the stuff—though he always found something insulting to say about the cereal whenever she thought fit to present him with it, just to annoy her and earn himself one of the earnest little lectures that always set him grinning and made her give that endearing little huff of impatience with what she had to see as his cussedness.

Always honest with himself, he had no choice but to admit that his reaction had everything to do with the way her breasts looked like ripe delicious melons encased in something blue, silky and clingy, the deep V neckline revealing a tantalising glimpse of breath-catching cleavage as she bent over him, the hint of subtle perfume she was wearing making his head spin.

He'd woken this morning more than half convinced that the notion that Howard, dumpy frumpy Howard, had turned into one fantastically desirable woman had been a mirage, a dream. But here and now the change in her—an impossible change he would have said—

was being impressed on his openly roaming, appreciative eyes.

She straightened, holding the empty tray against a curvy hip cocooned in sober dark blue. The colour was the only sober thing about a narrow skirt that lovingly skimmed ripe throat-tightening hips and was short enough to display shapely calves and neat ankles.

His eyes travelled slowly back up to where the silky stuff of the top she was wearing clung so lovingly to her tiny waist, on and up to the twin bountiful globes, the long creamy neck and cute face. He met her startlingly blue eyes, eyes to drown in, felt the hot, hard shock of physical desire punch his gut, wrenched his own eyes away and reached for the coffee pot.

His hand was shaking. *Santo cielo!* This had to stop! A man couldn't seduce his housekeeper and still expect his home life to run on an even keel! An affair with her would be domestic disaster. She might even pack her bags and walk out on him when the inevitable end came and he would have lost the best, most entertaining housekeeper he could ever hope to find.

'I don't know what time I'll be back this evening, Howard. Don't make supper and don't wait up.'

He swallowed his coffee. It scalded his mouth. Did nothing for his temper. Maybe his voice had emerged more harshly than he'd intended. He'd heard her sharp intake of breath at his curt dismissal. Something unrecognisable squeezed tightly around his heart. For the first time ever in his dealings with a female he felt like an uncouth brute! He clamped his mouth firmly shut on the instinctive apology that would put

them back on the old friendly, interestingly feisty
footing.

Distancing himself from her too-tempting new self
had to be the name of the game from now on, even
if, regrettably, his attitude towards her got to be colder
than an arctic winter.

His quicksilver mind grasped at the direction he
needed to follow. Jake Ferris and his wife, Janice—
long-standing friends—had issued an open-ended invitation to dine at their club to be introduced to some
woman or other who, Jake had confided, had been so
anxious to meet him she was practically drooling.
Now was the time to take the invitation up.

A new woman—and Jake had more sense than to
introduce him to a female less than fabulous—would
take his mind off temptations too near to home!

He dipped his spoon into the cereal, thankful to
note that his hand was steady again and Howard, still
hovering at his side, too close for his peace of mind,
cleared her throat.

'As you won't be needing me this evening, would
you mind if I invited a girl friend over for an hour?'

Mercy had no idea what had rattled his cage this
morning and she did her best to tell herself she didn't
much care. The darn man was beginning to mean too
much to her and she could only deplore that state of
affairs.

For instance, his grumpy statement that now he was
back from the business trip to Rome she had to forget
everything but dancing attendance on him, reinforcing
her subservient position, had really, really hurt, although she knew it shouldn't. She knew she was in
a subservient position, didn't she?

But he seemed to have the knack of knocking her back hard whenever he turned on that wicked charm and made her feel all gooey and melty inside—half way to believing that he regarded her as an equal, someone whose company he enjoyed—and that was just as insulting, hurtful and squashing as the way he had cast her in that humiliating commercial. She felt—well, the only way she could describe it was bleak and quite thoroughly flattened.

She would have slipped away when he'd snapped at her but Carly had been repeatedly pressing for an invite and his absence this evening presented the perfect opportunity. But she didn't know how she would explain it if Andreo's bad mood made him veto the idea of having any friend of his hired help sully the exclusive atmosphere of his beautiful home, so when he coldly delivered, 'If you must, Howard,' and opened his newspaper with a decided crackle and snap she turned on her heel and made herself scarce.

He hadn't meant to turn and watch her departure but he found himself somehow doing just that and, what was even worse, mentally applauding the sway of her delectable backside, noting with a surge of heat that the figure-hugging navy skirt had an eyecatching split up the back, affording a tantalising glimpse of—

Basta! He jack-knifed to his feet, dropping his unread paper over his uneaten cereal, and strode to the door, his jaw clamped so tight it made his teeth ache. The moment he hit his office he would phone Jake and accept the dinner invitation, insist on arranging it for this evening. And hope the drooling female was fanciable and fascinating enough to take his lustful thoughts away from Howard!

* * *

Vacuum cleaning and dusting all morning took Mercy's mind off her boss. Or that had been the general idea, she admitted as she half-heartedly made herself a scratch lunch. But however hard she tried she couldn't help the intrusion of thoughts centred around her muddled emotions.

Why did she let his mere presence excite her beyond sense or bearing? Why did he persistently stalk through her dreams every single night? Why did she fall asleep fantasising about being in his arms, that sensual mouth finding hers and claiming it? Why was her first waking thought always of him?

Why torture herself when he was way out of her league, and quite definitely not the type of man she would ever choose to commit herself to in any case because no girl with an ounce of sense in her head fell in love with a serial womanizer?

Why, when he didn't even see her except as part of the fixtures and fittings, when he hadn't even noticed her more attractive appearance, merely commenting offhandedly on the fact that she'd had her hair cut—as if she'd dropped into the nearest back street barber and not had one of the most sought-after stylists spending absolutely ages over the expert shaping and taming of that wild mop?

Pushing aside her now unwanted tuna salad, Mercy told herself firmly to snap out of it. Grow up. Think of something else.

She'd led a sheltered life, she would be the first to admit it; her social graces were non-existent, especially when it came to members of the opposite sex. It was no wonder that her first encounter with a guy as exotic as Andreo Pascali had put silly thoughts into her head.

A sigh dredged up from her toes. She had to put her boss's effect on her right out of her mind. Think of something else.

Like: Carly had accepted the invitation to come over this evening like a shot and that was something to look forward to. They would have the house to themselves, without her boss's demanding, all pervasive presence, and maybe, just maybe, she could swallow her pride and confide her difficulty to her friend and beg for her advice on the best way to get over her ridiculous crush. Because that was all it was, wasn't it?

She rose from the table, a frown clouding her brow. There she went again! Thinking of him when she'd been so determined not to do anything of the kind!

Her shoulders rigid with the effort to wipe all thoughts of Andreo Pascali from her consciousness, she exited the kitchen and mounted the stairs to her own quarters, changed into the new cream leggings patterned with scarlet poppies, topped it with a scarlet T-shirt that flattered her too-generous figure and took herself out to buy a bottle of the white wine Carly preferred. She was absolutely set on getting over her regrettable fixation on the wretched man because, if she didn't, this juvenile crush could develop into something far more dangerous, such as falling for him like a ton of bricks, because if that happened she would have to hand in her notice. And she would never find another job that paid as well.

As the taxi weaved through the mid-evening traffic Andreo's headache began, a million spiteful hammers pounding the inside of his skull. With a grunt of exasperation he undid the top buttons of his shirt and loosened his tie. He was too damn hot. And the whole wretched evening had been a total waste of time.

Jake had been his usual laid back self, Janice bubbly and fun to be with, and the female who had apparently been dying for an introduction—one of Janice's many friends—had been a tall, classy brunette with golden sultry eyes, a gold-coloured dress that had shown off her svelte figure to perfection and the ego-flattering knack of hanging on his every word.

Only his ego didn't need flattering and her come-bed-me eyes had left him cold. And edgy. Wanting out. This type of sexual charade suddenly sickened him. He had no interest in embarking on another affair. They were always fairly short-lived because his boredom threshold was low. The idea was distasteful. He should never have agreed to meet with the woman whose name now escaped him.

He'd made his excuses and left as the waiter handed out the dessert menus and tomorrow he'd have to call Janice and apologise for his ill manners and grovel.

All he'd wanted to do was get home, he admitted to himself as he let himself into the vast shadowy hall and quietly closed the heavy door behind him without his normal boundless energy. He'd never felt that way before. Home was a convenience, a place he was out of far more than he was in it.

And now he was burning up. Impatiently struggling out of his suit jacket, he lobbed it at a chair. Missed. Left it lying there and, driven by an instinct he didn't bother to examine, he raised his pounding head and called for Howard. But his voice came out as a mere rusty croak. His throat was rough and sore, on fire.

Scowling darkly, he gave in to the inevitable and began to mount the stairs. Slowly. He would have to go up and root her out. The way he was feeling, hot then cold, aching all over, his legs annoyingly shaky, had to mean he was coming down with something.

He was never ill!

He wouldn't put up with it!

He paused outside the door to Howard's self-contained apartment to snatch his breath back then felt his whole body go icy cold as he heard a male voice saying something and then laughing, a low husky sound that made all the hairs on his nape stand on end before producing a hot tide of blistering anger.

She'd lied! If that was a girlfriend she was entertaining in there then he was the Queen of England! He'd stamp right in and throw the guy out. Right out!

And tell Howard to pack her bags. Right now! He would take a certain amount of insubordination from her but he would not be lied to!

But his hand slicked off the moulded brass door knob. He was sweating like a pig, he noted with deep self-loathing. Too feeble to throw anyone bigger than an ant out of anywhere!

The thought of tottering through that door—all feeble limbs, croaky voice and sweaty brow—was totally abhorrent. He'd look a weak fool. A laughing stock.

Dio mio, he would never do that to himself, show himself as being less than in total control.

He would sack Howard first thing in the morning.

On that dire mental threat, he staggered back to his

own room, kicked off his shoes and spreadeagled his aching body on the bed, venting a groan as he wildly and painfully pictured what that guy was doing to the lushly seductive lying little minx right now.

CHAPTER SIX

MERCY woke on the dot of six as usual. Warm sun-
light streamed into the room and the large house was
silent.

Too silent.

What had happened to the usual early morning
whirlwind, Andreo rushing out for his early morning
run, the exuberant slam of the main door as he left—
cue for her to be up and busy and waiting for the
racket that would tell her he was back home and heading for his shower, sometimes singing something in
Italian at the top of his rich, melodious voice—cue
for her to start making his breakfast?

Remembering that he'd informed her that he had
no idea how late he'd be last night, and the brutal
delivery that had hurt her almost to the point of tears,
she decided he'd probably overslept.

Serve him right if she let him sleep until tomorrow
morning! was her initial unworthy thought as she
dressed in the poppy-splashed leggings and scarlet top
that had drawn an admiring wolf-whistle from Darren
last night.

She would have to hammer on Andreo's door to
wake him. Not to do so would be mean-spirited and
a dereliction of her housekeeperly duty, she told herself sensibly. He wasn't to know how easily he could
knock her back, hurt her feelings. And that was her
own fault entirely for harbouring a secret schoolgirl

crush on a man who obviously believed she could take whatever he threw at her with sublime indifference as she contemplated her generous pay packet!

Unfortunately Carly had brought Darren along with her, so she hadn't been able to confide in her friend and ask for her advice. But maybe it had been for the best, she decided as she trotted to the next storey down, heading for her boss's room. Carly would, quite rightly, have said she was a fool. Mercy could do without that being pointed out and she was quite capable and sensible enough to get over it all on her own.

Repeated hammerings on his door brought no response. Mercy's stomach churned as she took in the implications of the answering silence. Dispiritedly, she headed down the final flight of stairs, drawing the sickening and inevitable conclusion that he had failed to come home at all. Doubtless he had spent the night with some new woman—someone beautiful, sophisticated and worldly-wise, a replacement for the discarded Trisha.

But the first thing she saw as she gained the hall was his jacket, dumped on the floor.

Her first crazily happy thought was that he was back and not getting all close and personal with a new woman! The second was that he had risen earlier than usual and was already out, lured by the early sunshine.

She picked up the jacket and shook it out with a disapproving cluck, draping it over the back of a chair to be collected later, refusing to allow her fingers to do anything as soppy and sentimental as stroke the superb silk and alpaca fabric, although, annoyingly they itched to do just that. She headed for the kitchen to assemble the makings of his breakfast—half a grapefruit and mushrooms on toast today—and waited for the unmissable sounds of his return.

And waited.

At eight-fifteen she was sure something was wrong. However unpredictable he might be, in all other respects his morning routine never failed to operate like clockwork. His early run, his shower, breakfast on the stroke of eight and out of the house or into his home office by this time at the latest.

Eight-twenty.

Pulling in a deep breath, Mercy headed back up to his room and marched straight in, her heart doing a nosedive when she saw him sprawled out on the bed, fully clothed, apart from the discarded suit jacket.

His breathing was heavy enough for him to be dead drunk. But, although he enjoyed a glass of red wine, she had never seen him over-indulge. Although there was always a first time, she told herself, wondering whether to leave him to sleep it off.

He gave a groan and rolled over on to his back, arms outflung. Mercy approached the bedside briskly and laid a cool hand on his brow. The burning heat told her he was running quite a temperature. Not drunk. Ill. Her stomach lurched painfully.

One feverish eye opened. 'What time is it?'

'Gone eight.'

With growing concern she watched him struggle to sit up, sweat sheening his face, biting her lip as he said croakily, 'Should have left by now. Bring me black coffee.'

The gentlest pressure against his shoulder was

enough to have him collapsing back against the pillows. 'You're not well. You won't be going anywhere today,' Mercy told him firmly. 'Stay put. I'll bring you something to drink.'

Making him more comfortable could wait a few more minutes. Her priority was to phone his doctor. A sharp anxiety for him had her reaching the kitchen in record time, leafing through the notebook his previous housekeeper had filled with useful contact numbers and punching in the numbers of his doctor's surgery.

Receiving the comforting assurance that Doctor Allingham would be in attendance within the next half an hour, Mercy's heart settled down to a slower beat as she cogitated that he had to be a private patient because someone less privileged would have been told to get himself to the surgery or wait his turn in a long line for a house call.

'I'll be late in!' Struggling to sit up again, the rasping complaint hit her as soon as she re-entered the room. A split second later he collapsed in a grumpy heap against the pillows and Mercy, not letting him guess how concerned she was, removed his shoes and told him, 'I've already told you, you won't be working today. Tell me who to ask for and I'll phone through and explain after the doctor's seen you.'

'Don't need a doctor, wretched woman!' Andreo launched at her with blistering heat. Then, as if the violently expressed objection had exhausted him, his eyes suddenly closed, the ridiculously long lashes making smudgy dark crescents against his ashen moist skin.

Seriously alarmed and hating to see him like this

when he was usually bristling with energy, Mercy practically galloped for the *en suite* bathroom, filled a glass with water from the cold tap and nudged a space for herself on the bed beside him.

Slipping an arm beneath his shoulders, she raised his head and said tenderly, 'Drink this.' He was burning up; she could feel his blistering body heat through the sweat-soaked fabric of his shirt. Wondering whether there would be time to persuade him to get into fresh pyjamas before the doctor arrived, she held the glass to his lips and tried to ignore the sheet of lightning that hit home deep in her pelvis as his face nuzzled against her breast.

Feeling the cool glass against his parched lips, Andreo opened one eye. A scarlet top today. The firm warmth of her breast was *magnifica*! He nuzzled closer. Obediently, he took a sip of water then turned his aching head into the valley between her glorious breasts. And felt a whole heap better. His body stirred, there was no doubt about the insistence of what was happening. He burrowed deeper. *Questo maledetto!* If he didn't feel so weak he would ease her fully on to the bed and undress her slowly, kiss every inch of her divine body, make passionate love to her and let the consequences go hang!

Mercy sucked in a frantic breath as her breasts surged against the confines of the lacy bra she was wearing beneath the silky top and fiery heat flooded through her. Her throat closed up in panic. Could he tell what was happening to her? Did he know what he was doing to her? Oh, she did so hope not!

Involuntarily, the arm that was supporting his wide shoulders tightened, drawing him closer, although she surely hadn't consciously meant that to happen. Andreo made a dark, roughened, pleasured sound at the back of his throat and Mercy's breath caught. She had fantasised about this close intimacy, secretly and deplorably craved it so much that now it was actually happening she couldn't think straight, every last cell in her body too excited to harbour even the tiniest vestige of common sense.

Her dazed eyes were fixed on the top of his dark, rumpled head. Her lips wanted to follow but she stoically clamped them tight against her teeth, her heart swelling painfully at his far-from-the-norm vulnerability.

Maybe she had overreacted in calling his doctor. But she had to admit that she would move heaven and earth to have him fit and well again. She simply couldn't bear to see him felled by illness, all that dynamic energy of his wiped away, those laughing eyes glittering with fever.

Because she had grown to really care about him. Warts and all.

Because she loved him with all of her heart and soul!

The shattering self-knowledge dealt her a desperately savage blow, taking her breath away with the sheer enormity of it. Closing her eyes, she tried to get her head around the shocking revelation, scornfully dismiss it as unmitigated silliness. But she stopped trying when she knew she couldn't.

She hadn't wanted this to happen, had fought hard against it, had endlessly lectured herself on the folly of falling for a man who, like a spoiled toddler, re-

garded women as playthings to be discarded as soon
as he lost interest.

But it had happened anyway, and she was going to
have to deal with it, she decided sickly. Somehow.
And having his head between her almost painfully
sensitised breasts wasn't helping any. The awful sense
of loss when she pulled herself together, did the right
and proper thing and gently settled his head back on
the pillows, made herself despise herself for her
weakness and, shamingly, her voice was thick with
the knowledge of her love for him as she excused
herself. 'The doctor should be here shortly. I should
go down and wait.' She wondered whether the groan
he gave as she straightened up meant he'd enjoyed
being up close and cuddled or whether, and this was
far more likely, he still thought she'd overstepped the
mark in seeking the medical attention his macho-male
tendencies told him he did not want or need.

The latter, probably, she decided sensibly, absolutely determined to deny her newly raw emotions
anything at all to feed on.

'Flu,' Doctor Allingham told Mercy as he closed the
bedroom door behind him. 'Signor Pascali is strong
and fit so there should be nothing to worry about.'

Hovering outside the door, shifting agitatedly from
one foot to the other as she waited, Mercy knew her
eyes must look like saucers. The short, dapper, no-
nonsense medico must think she was a right air-brain,
judging from the way he'd lifted one bushy eyebrow
when she'd introduced herself as Signor Pascali's
housekeeper.

And here she was, hanging on his every word as if

they were facing a life and death situation instead of something as commonplace as influenza as he intoned, 'An out of season particularly virulent strain. I've seen two or three cases already. I've left tablets to help bring his temperature down. Four a day, see he takes them. Plenty to drink. And if he should experience breathing difficulties, contact me at once. I'll see myself out. Good day to you.'

Mercy made a conscious effort to relax the frown of concentration from her brow as she watched him begin to descend the stairs and then stiffened her spine as she re-entered the sick room. She didn't want to be in love with him and self-preservation demanded that she have as little to do with him as possible but she would do her best to care for him, strictly in the line of duty, she told herself, while knowing that wild horses wouldn't keep her from his side while he was ill and needed her.

Avoid eye contact. Keep calm and aloof. Above all, don't get close, and any touchy-feely stuff was out. Definitely out. The first stringent steps in schooling herself to fall out of love with such an unsuitable guy.

Sensible resolutions that took an immediate and sharp nosedive when he grunted, 'Help me out of my clothes.'

Her soft heart stopped the tart rejoinder, I'm sure you can manage if you put your mind to it. Propped up on one elbow, fumbling weakly with his shirt buttons and getting nowhere, those silvery eyes darkening with appeal, what else could she do?

It was an almighty struggle to haul his dead weight semi-upright while she stripped off his sodden shirt,

enforcing close contact of the kind she had vowed to
avoid like the plague. That couldn't be a gleam of
pure wickedness she had glimpsed beneath partly
lowered thick black lashes. Just the fever.

And the shamingly husky note in her voice when
she handed him the water glass and a tablet saying,
'Take this,' was just the result of her exertions and
nothing to do with the sleek olive-toned skin on those
wide shoulders, the defining muscles of a torso that
arrowed down to a flat stomach and a narrow waist
that disappeared beneath the band of the crumpled
suit trousers.

She wouldn't let it be!

'Pyjamas?' Her heart was thumping. She handled
his laundry as part of her job. She knew he must sleep
in his skin. But surely he had a pair somewhere, if
only for emergencies?

'Never use them.'

With a frown of concentration he was pushing ir-
ritably at the waistline of his trousers.

Mercy's throat closed right up and her heart galloped as she mentally bowed to the inevitable,
screwed her eyes shut and felt for the fastening and
pulled down the zipper, the backs of her fingers coming into unlooked-for, unwanted sizzling contact with
the hair-roughened skin, making her tremble and her
face turn—she was humiliatingly sure of this—a horrible brick-red.

The trousers successfully round his ankles, she
peeped between her lashes because working blind was
difficult. The trousers disposed of, she could smartly
cover him up with the duvet that he'd obviously

kicked aside and now billowed over the foot of the bed.

Only one obstacle remained. Silk boxer shorts. As soaked with sweat as his shirt had been. Gritting her teeth, trying to pull air into her oxygen-starved lungs, Mercy gripped the damp silk and tugged.

It was an Oh-My-God! moment. Her skin boiled and her legs turned to water and Andreo got out—with hoarse amusement? 'Never seen a naked man before, Howard?'

Mercy wanted to slap him! To put her fingers round his throat and throttle him for being what he was, who he was, for making her love him, want him, really, really care about him!

Hauling herself together, she covered him with the lightweight duvet, gathered his discarded clothing to be dealt with later and told him with apparent off-handedness, no big deal, 'Of course I have. Dozens of times.'

Her brother James was male, wasn't he? She'd often helped her mother bath him when he was a toddler, so she wasn't lying, was she?

Satisfied that she had held her own, robbed him of any amusement he might have gained from taking it into his far too handsome head that she had never been in the position to lay eyes on the naked male body, never even had a boyfriend—which she hadn't but he wasn't going to know that—she swept from the room, calling, 'I'll bring you a glass of juice and then you must try to sleep.'

Back in the kitchen, one hand clutching the glass of orange juice she'd just poured, Mercy just stood there, staring into space. The revelation of how she really felt about her impossible boss had shattered her. And somehow she was going to have to work her muddled, understandably over-emotional way through it.

She was famous for being sensible, wasn't she? Now was the time to live up to that reputation. And then some. Handing in her notice while he was unwell was out of the question; her conscience wouldn't let her. But as soon as he was on his feet she would do just that and hope to goodness she could find another job and somewhere to live and then she could begin the process of forgetting she'd ever laid eyes on him, fallen head over heels in love with him. It was the only sensible thing to do.

Galvanised into belated action by the much needed shot of common sense, she was halfway back up the stairs when she tottered to an appalled standstill.

How could she put self-preservation above James's financial welfare?

The odds against her landing such a well-paid live-in job in the immediate future, if ever, were about a trillion to one! And she'd have to shell out the best part of a fortune on rent for somewhere even halfway decent to live.

How could she be so selfish?

Provided she didn't do or say something to earn herself the sack, she would have to grit her teeth and stay put and endure the pain of loving someone who would never love her back because women, to him, came into the category of light entertainment. When he settled down and married it wouldn't be for love but for a fortune that, even if it didn't match his own, was very nice thank you. A cynical lifeplan he'd expounded himself.

So she'd have to stay here, at least until James was qualified and earning.

On that decidedly challenging and sobering thought she entered his room, placed the glass of juice on the night table and was turning away with a commendably distant, 'Drink it. Doctor's orders,' when he grimaced and reached for her hand.

'Stay, Mercy. Make me warm.'

His teeth were actually chattering, Mercy noted with a searing pang, her loving heart going straight out to him as she took in his pallor, the trembling of his impressive frame. The virus was hitting him badly. She had to do something to help him.

Dismissing the time-wasting chore of filling a dozen hot water bottles—and going out to buy them in the first place because she certainly hadn't come across any such item during her time here—as a complete non-starter, she again bowed to the inevitable, drew back a corner of the duvet and slipped in beside him, wrapping her arms round his shaking body with a sense of deep shame for the wicked stab of sexual delight that coursed right the way through her as he melted into the warmth of her body with a grunt of pleasure and buried his head between her breasts.

Cradling his naked body in her arms, her hands splayed out against the satiny smooth skin that covered his shaking bones, was sheer unmitigated torture. She was lost in a vortex of hot excitement, a hitherto unknown sexual excitement that could never be assuaged because it was so wrong for her.

In normal circumstances this would never have

happened—had he implied what he had and mentioned her name in the same breath, she would have hit the ground at a run and still been running—she tried to console herself, needing all the excuses she could summon up. But he was out of his skull with fever and he wasn't to know that her need was so huge and immediate that she was in danger of losing what was left of her sanity, her self-respect and her moral certainties! At least she could take some comfort from that, from knowing that, of the two of them, only she knew how stupid she was.

Smothering a groan, Mercy promised herself that as soon as he stopped shivering she would smartly extricate herself from this far too intimate embrace and remove herself to take a long, very cold shower.

She couldn't wait. But she would have to because he was burrowing even closer into the warmth of her generous curves, one leg flung over hers now, and he was muttering disjointedly in his own language.

He was delirious, she decided, desperately worried for him, her concern for the man she was unfortunate enough to have fallen in love with obliterating her self-protective need to make herself scarce. She lifted her hands and smoothed his raven-dark, rumpled hair away from his burning forehead, aching inside with her need to make him feel better. Perhaps a cold damp cloth would dissipate some of that burning heat. But her intention to fetch one was stymied as soon as she attempted to slide off the bed as one surpisingly strong arm anchored her to the mattress.

A plea she was powerless to resist, she admitted weakly, biting her lip as he snuggled closer and settled his head against hers with a satisfied grunt. As if they were a loving married couple, she thought, swallowing a riven sob. But he was out of it. He didn't know what he was doing; he only instinctively sought human comfort—almost anyone would have done— it was nothing personal for him.

For her it was far too personal but she would just have to grit her teeth and bear it because, for her, his needs came first. Always.

A solitary tear rolled down her cheek. Resigning herself to the position she found herself in, she viewed with equal quantities of pain and pleasure the hours that had to pass before his next medication was due, thankful that at long last he seemed to have slipped into peaceful sleep.

Time seemed to stand still. His breathing was lighter, his closeness a torment. The warmth of that magnificently lithe, naked all-male body so intimately connected to hers seared straight through the barrier of her clothes to her skin, setting her on fire, no matter how staunchly she tried to ignore the unnerving sensation.

Maybe it would be okay to slip away now? He seemed really peaceful at last. And then he stirred in his sleep, both his hands unerringly moving to slide beneath her top to cup her breasts. Catching her breath on a silent sob, Mercy felt her flesh harden, press against the mind-shaking warmth of his possessive palms and knew she just had to make herself move away. And for the life of her she couldn't. The slow, seductive way his hands were shaping her, his murmured, 'Bella, bella...' blotted out everything but the exquisite sensation, sending a fierce drum-beat of desire crashing through her.

She had to do something to stop this. Move. Get off this bed. He was delirious, didn't know what he was doing.

But she did!

She was so ashamed of herself!

And then he kissed her, his mouth drawing a response from her that she hadn't known she could give, all her earlier moralising blown away on a storm of frantic, hot excitement where nothing mattered but what was happening and the heavy thud of his heartbeat against the wild pattering of her own.

CHAPTER SEVEN

MERCY sat at the kitchen table, staring despondently at the mug of coffee she'd made and now didn't want, trying her level best to be calm and sensible about the shattering situation she now found herself in. A vitally necessary task, but almost impossible when her entire body was still aching for Andreo, desperately needing him to finish what he'd started!

Just remembering how shamelessly, and let's face it—greedily, she had clung to him—actually squirmed and wriggled against him—inhibitions about what was right and proper heedlessly scattered to the four winds as she'd found that wide sensual mouth again at the very same moment he withdrew the sheer magic he was creating, just adoring the way he so swiftly and eagerly responded, as if he could never get enough of her—was enough to make her face turn scarlet with shame.

Forcing herself to punishingly recall the mortifying horror of how she had so feverishly matched the way his hands were shaping her body by avidly exploring his and discovering to her wildly elated shock that he was hugely aroused, made her feel decidedly unwell in retrospect, and knowing that her shamefully eager hands had already been pushing frantically at the waistband of her leggings made her feel so very much worse.

How could she have behaved like such an out-and-

Get FREE BOOKS and a FREE GIFT when you play the...

LAS VEGAS
GAME

Just scratch off the gold box with a coin. Then check below to see the gifts you get! →

YES! I have scratched off the gold box. Please send me my 2 FREE BOOKS and gift for which I qualify. I understand that I am under no obligation to purchase any books as explained on the back of this card.

▶ DETACH AND MAIL CARD TODAY! ▶

306 HDL EFZZ   106 HDL EFYQ

FIRST NAME   LAST NAME

ADDRESS

APT.#   CITY

STATE/PROV.   ZIP/POSTAL CODE   (H-P-08/06)

7	7	7	Worth TWO FREE BOOKS plus a BONUS Mystery Gift!
🍒	🍒	🍒	Worth TWO FREE BOOKS!
🔔	🔔	♣	TRY AGAIN!

www.eHarlequin.com

Offer limited to one per household and not valid to current Harlequin Presents® subscribers. All orders subject to approval.

Your Privacy - Harlequin is committed to protecting your privacy. Our policy is available online at www.eharlequin.com or upon request from the Harlequin Reader Service. From time to time we make our lists of customers available to reputable firms who may have a product or service of interest to you. If you would prefer for us not to share your nam

The Harlequin Reader Service® — Here's how it works:

Accepting your 2 free books and mystery gift places you under no obligation to buy anything. You may keep the books and gift and return the shipping statement marked "cancel." If you do not cancel, about a month later we'll send you 6 additional books and bill you just $3.80 each in the U.S., or $4.47 each in Canada, plus 25¢ shipping & handling per book and applicable taxes if any. * That's the complete price and — compared to cover prices of $4.50 each in the U.S. and $5.25 each in Canada — it's quite a bargain! You may cancel at any time, but if you choose to continue, every month we'll send you 6 more books, which you may either purchase at the discount price or return to us and cancel your subscription.

*Terms and prices subject to change without notice. Sales tax applicable in N.Y. Canadian residents will be charged applicable provincial taxes and GST. Credit or debit balances in a customer's account(s) may be offset by any other outstanding balance owed by or to the customer. Please allow 4 to 6 weeks for delivery.

If offer card is missing write to: Harlequin Reader Service, 3010 Walden Ave., P.O. Box 1867, Buffalo NY 14240-1867

BUSINESS REPLY MAIL
FIRST-CLASS MAIL   PERMIT NO. 717-003   BUFFALO, NY

POSTAGE WILL BE PAID BY ADDRESSEE

HARLEQUIN READER SERVICE
3010 WALDEN AVE
PO BOX 1867
BUFFALO NY 14240-9952

NO POSTAGE
NECESSARY
IF MAILED
IN THE
UNITED STATES

out trollop? she wondered helplessly as self-disgust beat at her in giant waves of shame. Her wanton behaviour flew in the face of everything her parents had taught her, not to mention her own firmly held opinion that sex without loving long-term commitment on both sides was debasing.

If she had to be in love with him—and at the moment there seemed to be no easy way out of that hopeless situation—then she had to learn to adore him in secret, saying nothing, doing nothing to clue him in to how she felt.

Had he not suddenly gone still then turned his back on her and fallen into a coma-like sleep—

Do not go there! She groaned sickly, taking a swift mental swipe at that cringe-making thought. Just give thanks that her guardian angel had flown in and helpfully poleaxed him before the inevitable conclusion!

She'd scrambled off that bed, her face on fire, and cringingly slunk away, feeling horrified at what could have happened—with her egging him on with the sort of lusty appetite that certainly didn't fit with what she thought she'd known of herself—only to have to force herself back up to his room again when it was time for his second dose of medication.

Not knowing whether he'd grab her for more of the same and whether she'd be strong enough to resist another slice of pure heaven had been a question of nightmare proportions. But she'd managed it, had gently shaken him awake, noting with the part of her mind that wasn't completely doolally that he actually looked less feverish, and urged him to take his tablet and drink all the water.

Thankfully, he'd complied with only a token grumble. Hadn't even looked at her, not directly. And, far from asking her not to leave him, he'd simply handed her the empty glass and turned his back to her.

Part of her had felt as if she'd been smacked in the eye but the sensible part, which was doing its utmost to assume the dominant role, had told her that his insulting dismissal—insulting, considering what had happened right on this bed an hour earlier—was a really good sign.

Had he been so delirious he didn't remember a thing? It was a hope. One that gathered a comforting momentum. A hope she was clinging on to with all her might because, if she was wrong and he did remember, she would never be able to look him in the face ever again.

Propped up against the pillows, his hands hooked behind his head, Andreo congratulated himself on the clarity of his forward thinking.

He'd wanted his lush, curvy housekeeper with every atom of his being. He'd never, ever, wanted a woman that desperately. The way she'd responded to him had been out of this world, something he was damned if he'd do without just because he didn't want to lose the best housekeeper he was ever likely to find.

There was no solid reason he could now think of to count against his newly born conviction that, with care on his part, she could be persuaded to take on both roles. Housekeeper and mistress.

A smile of anticipation warmed the dark silver of his eyes. No reason. But he would have to move with very great care. Despite her response to him more than living up to the promise of her fabulous body, she was a moral little soul. She could probably write off one fall from grace as a deeply regrettable aberration, never to be repeated, but a long-term live-in mistress—no, her moral upbringing would make her draw the line at that unless he worked hard at convincing her otherwise.

It would be a first for him, a challenge to be relished. Never in his life had he had to work at wooing a woman. He usually had to fight them off, rejecting far more than he ever chose.

It had begun to bore him!

Howard, even in her frumpy dumpy persona, had never bored him!

He could see her lasting far longer than the usual handful of weeks! He shifted restively. How much longer before she made him take another tablet? He wanted her here, now. But he had to remember his strategy.

He must not rush things.

He recalled how she'd looked when she handed him that last pill—chastened, embarrassed, edgy, ready to run screaming from the room if he so much as smiled at her! He would have to call on all his self-restraint and quieten her as he would quieten a spooked mare until she was eating out of his hand.

Thanking his lucky stars that he'd had the sense to pull back when they'd both teetered on the brink of the point of no return—partly, he had to admit, down to his feeling that in his enfeebled state he would be unable to perform at the peak of his ability—he had feigned sleep and plotted his next moves.

The most pressing of which was to get her away

from here. Away from the guy she'd been entertaining in her room—probably with cocoa and biscuits, knowing her! He'd been hopping mad at the time, vowing to sack her for some warped reason that was probably down to the way he'd been feeling at the time. Rotten.

And he could discount her probably wild exaggeration about how many male nudes she'd seen. If she had made love with some guy it must have been because the lying creep had promised her a wedding ring! Whatever happened, he would never lie to her. He would never hurt her; she was far too special to him.

On that complacent thought he settled himself to wait.

The room was in darkness when Mercy entered. Determined to set the tone, act as if nothing had happened, she flicked on the overhead light and chirped, 'Tablet time—and I've heated up some soup.'

Holding her breath, she waited for his response. A lascivious leer? An invitation to join him in the bed, to carry on where they'd left off? Or would he have no memory of her disgraceful behaviour?

Andreo gave her a calculated sour look, lurched over on his side and dragged the duvet up over his shoulders. 'Don't want it!'

Mercy let out her pent-up breath on a puff of relief. It was the sort of response she'd been praying for. He was back to normal—no uncharacteristic clinginess, no begging her to stay and make him warm! It really did look as if she was off the hook, her blushes spared! If he had any hazy memory of what had hap-

pened he would put it down to a delirium-fuelled
dream.

'Don't be difficult!' she chided softly as she shook
a tablet out of the bottle and handed it to him, passing
him the water. 'At least make the effort.'

'Bully!' A ghost of a smile curved that sensual
mouth and, knowing that her feeble heart was on the
brink of melting to an unwanted state of gooey mush,
she sped over the polished boards to lower the ve-
netian blinds and close out the night sky. When at last
she turned, taking far longer than necessary over the
simple task, Andreo was sitting up against the pillows, holding the soup, pushing the spoon around the
bowl.

'Sorry, Howard. Just can't face eating anything.
Wretched flu! I'll be fine by tomorrow. In any case,
I think I need a real break. You know what they say
about all work and no play—'

The gleam in his eyes made her own temperature
rise. He might be livid because a virus had had the
gross temerity to sap him of all that vital energy but
that didn't stop the charismatic seductive glimmer in
those fabulous eyes.

He probably didn't even know he was doing it and
surely she could handle that, no problem! But her
loving heart squeezed painfully as she fought the instinct to give him a cuddle, assure him that he was
doing fine, would soon be fighting fit again.

Touching him, getting all close and personal, was
something she definitely couldn't handle. Been there,
done that, and it had been a near disaster!

She took the bowl, which now looked in danger of
depositing its contents all over the duvet which was

rucked up around his narrow hips. Tearing her eyes from the expanse of that perfectly honed male torso, she hardened her heart and, trying hard to forget how much she loved him and ached to comfort and cosset him, she said snippily, 'No problem. You'll eat when you're hungry. In the meantime, if there's nothing you need, I'll say goodnight.' And escaped before he could think of something.

After a night largely spent giving herself a good talking to and stalwartly convincing herself that he didn't recall what had happened between them, Mercy felt just a little less jittery.

On her foray into the sick room, bearing a tray with juice and a plate of scrambled eggs garnished with tiny triangles of hot buttered toast, Mercy was presented with the sight of Andreo, dressed in jeans and a faded old T-shirt tottering around the room like a ninety-year-old in a drunken stupor.

'Trying my legs out,' he huffed, determinedly not looking into those huge sparkling azure eyes that had widened, almost filling her gorgeous face. 'Feel as if the damn things don't belong to me so I'll exercise them until they do!' he grouched.

Steeling every sinew in her body, Mercy forced herself not to rush like a lovesick ninny to help him. Seeing him like this made a tight lump form in her throat. Swallowing around it, she told him as matter-of-factly as she could, 'Sit in that chair and have your breakfast,' and watched him comply when she'd fully expected him to say he didn't want it, landing her with a full-scale rebellion.

Settling the tray on his lap, she made the mistake

of looking into his wickedly handsome face and felt
everything inside her quiver. At least he'd got most
of his colour back, she thought prosaically, determined to ignore the way her whole body leapt to
stinging life when she was near to him. But how he
made those lively silver eyes look quite so blank she
didn't know and, not able to help herself, she consoled him softly, 'You're doing brilliantly. But don't
push it. You were very ill but the medication's working—plus you've got the constitution of an ox, and if
you're sensible and take things steadily and eat as
much as you can manage you'll soon be back on your
feet.'

Pushing a tiny triangle of toast into his mouth, not
only because he was suddenly ravenous but seeing it
as the best way to prevent a huge grin breaking out
because he adored it when she put on that delightfully
earnest expression and delivered one of her little hom-
ilies—always had—he noted that this morning she
was wearing one of the voluminous grey overalls,
which confirmed his opinion that she was embarrassed and appalled by what they'd shared right there
on that bed. She had put it on like a suit of armour
and his heart melted. Poor little darling! He would
have to teach her that physical desire was nothing to
be ashamed of.

Cataclysmic physical desire in his case.

Watching her bustle about, changing his bedlinen,
he felt all the bones in his body soften. That grey
tent-like thing was no armour at all, not when he
could remember exactly, and in the clearest possible
detail, how her lush body had felt beneath his hands.

Doing his best to make his voice sound as matter-of-fact as he possibly could, he put the first part of his plan into action. 'Howard—' She straightened from scooping up an armful of discarded bedding, her lovely face tight with what he could only suppose was apprehension. 'Was I really that ill? Yesterday's a total blank.' He watched relief swamp her features and basked in the sudden warmth of her radiantly beautiful smile, knowing he'd struck exactly the right note if the second part of his plan was to work.

'You had a high fever. I think you were delirious most of the time.'

The relief was so immense she felt dizzy. He didn't remember a thing! The whole day—including those regrettable events—was a total blank! He would never know how his humble housekeeper had practically ravished him when all his defences were down! She wouldn't have to blush and cringe in his company and, provided she could act as if nothing had changed the status quo, she should be able to hang on to her dignity and her job and take very great care that he never had the slightest reason to guess how she felt about him.

'Another thing, Howard—' He longed for the day when he would lavish endearments on her but for now he had to tread gently. 'I've decided to take a long overdue break, visit my home on the Amalfi coast for a week or so. Pass me the phone—there'll be arrangements to make—and, when you've dealt with the laundry, bring me another drink.'

Successfully dismissing her, he punched in the numbers that would connect him to his other resident housekeeper, instructing the voluble little Italian woman to make herself scarce, take an extra unscheduled paid holiday—anywhere but Amalfi for at least two weeks.

Then felt immediately bad about it. Very bad. He was never devious but here he was, behaving like a particularly wily snake.

Telling himself that the end justified the means— no matter how personally distasteful those means were—he announced the moment she re-entered, 'The housekeeper at my Italian home is on leave. You'll have to come with me.'

He saw a rosy flush spread over her cheeks and knew, just knew, she was about to make a strong objection so before she could open her mouth and say what was obviously on her mind he tossed at her, 'Your job is to look after me and my home environment—wherever that happens to be. And as Sonniva will be away you will have to take her place.'

CHAPTER EIGHT

'So THIS is where you're hiding!'

Mercy's throat tightened convulsively as Andreo's rough velvet tones came from directly behind her. And her cheeks burned as she felt the betraying swelling of her breasts beneath the scanty protection of the very tiny top of the bikini he had personally picked out for her down on the coast on their first full day here in Italy. He'd insisted, 'You must look on this as a holiday, too. What is the use of the villa's swimming pool if it is not used? And don't argue! If you won't choose something for yourself, then I must!'

He couldn't have properly looked at what he'd selected, Mercy had decided charitably the first time she'd put it on, intending to take an afternoon dip. It was positively indecent. She'd taken it off in double quick time and, not able to completely resist the temptation of the sparkling blue pool, had taken to rising just before dawn while her boss was still safely asleep.

And now, drat it, he'd found her, wearing this embarrassing thing!

'You've enjoyed your swim?'

'Yes, very much.' She was sitting on the edge of the huge oval pool and she didn't want to turn and look at him, not when so much of her flesh was revealed. Not that it would affect him, of course, but it was already affecting her. Put her, within a whisker of being naked, next to the man she was unfortunately growing to love and want more with each second that passed and she wouldn't like to bet on her wretched hormones behaving themselves.

'I'll be in directly to fix breakfast,' she offered breathily, doing her best to sound dismissive.

Would the small towel that she'd been using to rough dry her hair cover her sufficiently if he didn't take the hint and make himself scarce while he waited for the coffee, crusty rolls and fresh figs and apricots he preferred for his first meal of the day?

'Today I have made breakfast. Come.' He was holding out a hand to assist her to her feet; Mercy could see it from the corner of her eye.

Knowing that to refuse to accept what had to be an innocuous and gentlemanly offer of help might make him just a little bit suspicious about the true state of her feelings for him, Mercy took his hand and be- tween quailing at the lightning electric charge that zipped all over her from the contact of his firm grasp, the touch of his warm dry skin on the palm of her hand and getting to her feet and trying to suck her tummy in at the same time as endeavouring to single- handedly cover some of herself with the tiny towel, she dropped it.

'You have a beautiful body; don't try to hide it.' Andreo retrieved the towel, held on to it, simmering silver eyes making an erotic, lingering sweep of shapely legs, the flare of her all-woman hips, the neat indentation of the waist beneath those glorious breasts, eventually fastening on the softness of her quivering mouth.

He ached to kiss her, to lose himself in her, but his

campaign called for finesse, not the sort of bull-at-a-gate tactics that would have her running for cover. She was too special to risk frightening her off with a false move.

When they made love she had to want it as much as he did, to be willing to share his bed and his life until the time came when they both recognised that it was time to call it a day, move on. But what they would have would be so precious that the day to end it seemed so far distant it was way out of sight. That conviction was a first for him and it tightened the breath in his lungs and brought his brows together in a perplexed spasm.

Dragging his eyes away, his fingers loosened reluctantly. He dropped her hand. 'Come.' He began to walk towards the villa, the white walls reflecting the radiance of the morning sun. 'I'll fix the coffee while you dress.'

Mercy vented a shivery sigh and followed on peculiarly unsteady legs, looking anywhere but at the virile figure ahead of her, clad this morning in narrow fawn denims and a stark black shirt.

Had he meant it when he'd said she had a beautiful body? Or had he been teasing, sensing her embarrassment, trying to put her at her ease because he was used to women like his fabulous ex-mistress who were proud of their bodies and not afraid of flaunting them?

At least he was now back to normal—as defined by the slightly distant but pleasant politeness of the past few days, ever since they'd arrived in Italy.

She'd agreed to come, partly because he'd said she must and he paid her wages, but mostly because he'd shown no sign of recalling the torrid episode in his bed and had spent his time working in his study while getting over the worst effects of the virus, only speaking to her when absolutely necessary.

But the way he'd looked at her just now, as if memorising every curve of her almost naked body, those devastatingly sexy eyes sliding over every quivering inch, had shaken her out of her sense of security, made her frantic with worrying over how on earth she would find the will-power to tell him to get lost if he decided he'd been without a woman for too long and needed a light holiday diversion. The way he'd looked at her had been so very explicit!

She loved him, wanted him, needed him. But no way would she be his sex toy! Her skin fluttered as if kissed by a thousand butterfly wings and unwelcome heat pooled between her thighs, signalling her appalling lack of will-power where her boss was concerned.

Thankfully, though, the way he was striding away without so much as a backward glance had to help to convince her that he was sticking to the employer/employee relationship and, hating herself for positively disliking what should be a huge consolation, she slipped into the villa by the main door while he headed for the gate in the walled courtyard and the kitchen regions.

Dressed in a cheap and cheerful cotton skirt and the silky blue top, Mercy forced herself down to the kitchen where she could hear Andreo whistling and the clattering of the chunky earthenware coffee cups.

As she entered—dragging in a breath that was

meant to steady her pattering heartbeats—he was adding the coffee pot to an already laden tray. The way
he looked up, soft dark hair falling over his forehead,
the smile he gave her making her tummy loop the
loop, almost had her turning tail and running for a
place of safety, as far away from the wicked temptation of him as she could get.

But she was made of sterner stuff. Deliberately
chirpy, she scolded, 'I'm supposed to housekeep.
That's what you pay me for,' she reminded briskly.
'Don't tell me you got me here under false pretences!'

The wrong thing to say! she railed at herself when
those sexy eyes held hers with stupefying intimacy as
he came back, 'And would you mind if I had?'

How was she supposed to answer that? A breathy,
Not at all!—a response that he probably would have
elicited from any other woman on the planet. But she
wasn't any woman, was she? She had moral integrity,
she enforced to herself, conveniently forgetting the
one occasion when she had shown none at all!

Mentally putting on her no-nonsense housekeeper's
hat, she remarked prosaically, 'Naturally. I would
strongly object to taking wages and not fulfilling my
duties.'

'I wonder…' His wide white grin drew her into his
magnetic spell, set danger signals clanging in her
brain as he lifted the heavy tray as if it weighed no
more than a fallen leaf. 'We breakfast outside.' He
exited by the courtyard door, placing the tray on the
sturdy wooden table beneath a vine-covered arbour.
'The weather is too good to waste and today is to be
a holiday for both of us. So tell me, what would you
like to do?' He held out a chair for her.

When she was seated she ignored her racing heart-beats and replied repressively, 'I thought I'd wash the kitchen floor.'

'An activity I, as your boss, forbid.' He poured coffee and handed her a cup. Then sat, long legs sprawled out, in the chair opposite, his smile pure temptation as he murmured, 'Today I spoil you and give myself pleasure in the process. We can drive down into Amalfi for lunch, make a day of it. Or relax here in the pool and in the shade beside it, together, talk a little—there is much I'd like to learn about you. And today we forget that I am your employer and that you wash my socks and dust my floors and become my beautiful angel of mercy when I am ill. Mercy—you were aptly named, is that not so?'

The devil was flirting with her! Just a little. Was he so bored by this, for him, unusual inactivity? Was his vital, restless spirit prompting him into looking for amusement at her expense?

Refusing to waste any more effort on trying to find answers, Mercy took a gulp of coffee and scalded her mouth and Andreo said, 'Decide which would most please you while we eat. There is no hurry; we have all the time in the world.'

Either choice was impossible, given the state of her emotions! Somehow she would have to wriggle out of going anywhere, doing anything, with him.

Watching those long tanned fingers deftly moving as he sliced into a fruit she felt her head spin, her breasts feeling tighter and heavier than usual, as she recalled how—unbeknown to him, thank heaven!—those hands had felt against her eager body, driving her wild and utterly wanton, wanting the seductive caresses to last for ever, wanting more, so very much more!

Mercy swallowed her mew of distress along with a corner of a crusty roll and wished she could forget. She knew she never would, and frantically viewed the options he had given her.

They'd driven down from the hills, past cultivated steep terraces, to Amalfi on their first day here and he'd insisted on buying that excuse for a swimsuit. It had been fun wandering through the ancient alleys and courtyards of the old town, exploring the cheerful seafront market. They had decided that the beach was too crowded to stroll on and Andreo had led her up into the town where they had lunched on delicious seafood.

He had been mostly silent—an unusual state of affairs that Mercy had put down to the after-effects of the flu. But today he was positively bristling with vitality again and she didn't think she could handle a whole day in his company with no escape route without her poor heart getting more mangled than it already was.

'I'd prefer to stay right here,' she announced, noting that he'd finished eating and was leaning back, one arm hooked over the back of his chair. Looking at her. With that devilish smile curving the corners of his sensual mouth.

Leaping to her feet, Mercy began stacking the used dishes on the tray, wishing she had packed the huge grey overalls because at least they gave her more housekeeperly gravitas. 'You wanted a holiday. So you go ahead and enjoy it. I have work to do.'

'Stop!' His hand shot out, long fingers fastening

around her wrist. 'You don't have to run from me.'
His thumb was stroking the tender skin of her inner
wrist. Mercy caught her breath, wanting to jerk her
hand away, knowing she should but, perversely, letting it stay exactly where it was because she craved
his touch with all her being.

'I am not your enemy,' he assured smokily.

The sheer sexiness of his delivery made her bones
melt but, self-protectively, she rose to the challenge
and parried, 'You are my boss. Sir. Nothing else.'

Just the love of my life!

She wanted to weep.

Still holding her wrist across the table, he rose to
his feet and drew her to his side. So close they were
almost touching. A shiver of sensation that was as
delicious as it was counter-productive took up residence down the length of her spine. The hand that
held her wrist loosened until it was more like a caress.
Mercy knew she should move away but couldn't
make herself and had to fight a terrible craving to inch
closer so that she could feel that magnificent body
touching hers, imprinting her flesh with the potent
virility of his.

'I could be...something else.'

Deliberately misunderstanding what had to be a def-
inite come-on and steeling herself to resist temptation
in whatever form it presented itself, Mercy removed
her hand from where he held it in a silken caress and
snapped, 'I'm sure you could be something other.'
Her chin came up. 'Well-behaved, for starters—given
the right tuition.'

A sudden stillness froze his features for just one
moment before his dark brows thundered down.

Hands planted on non-existent hips, he demanded, 'You accuse me of having no manners? Of ill behaviour?' Lushly lashed eyes burned down at her from his impressive height, his elegant blade of a nose pinched with deep displeasure.

Mercy choked on a hastily suppressed giggle. She couldn't have elicited more outraged pride had she accused the Pope of being a pimp! She had infuriated him and that look would have sent any other unfortunate lippy employee legging it for cover. But he couldn't frighten her. She grinned, she simply couldn't help it, and straightened her shoulders to meet whatever icily telling strictures he decided to throw at her.

Anger flowed out of him like bath water down a plughole. It was that glorious smile that did it. It always had done. It transformed an interestingly attractive young woman into a warm, excitingly seductive beauty. Heat bubbled unstoppably through his veins as Andreo decided patience was for wimps and consigned the softly-softly approach to kingdom come, took her fabulously sexy, gorgeous body in his arms and lowered his dark head.

He wanted her with a driven desperation that was entirely new to him, a desperation that had scattered his planned gentle seduction to the four corners of the earth. Groaning low in his throat, he deepened the kiss and his last semi-coherent thought, passing through his mind like a wispy cloud, was that no other woman, ever, had the power to make him jettison any plans he might have made, erasing every last vestige of his control and will.

As his mouth took hers Mercy stopped breathing.

Her heartbeat racing, she kissed him back and felt every sane thought she'd ever had melt away beyond recall. She was like a mindless doll where the man she loved was concerned, was her last joined-up thought before the hand that wasn't cradling her head slipped down to caress one full breast, pushing inside the deep V of the neckline to gain intimate access.

Mercy gasped out loud as every atom of her body quivered in ecstatic response and Andreo dragged his mouth from hers, his skin flushed as he told her fracturedly, 'I want you. All of you. In my life, at my side, in my bed.' His other hand took gentle possession of her other breast and Mercy could feel his body trembling as he added in a roughened undertone, 'Tell me you want this too, my beautiful angel!'

He was offering heaven. Mercy's body threatened meltdown before an icy shaft of reason shamed her.

Hell, more like, she renamed wildly. She struggled to rearrange her top, reclaim some modesty. A few weeks of heaven before the heartbreak of being sloughed off like a garment he'd become bored with. No regrets on his part. He'd had not a single one when he'd given Trisha her marching orders.

Forewarned was forearmed against future bitter heartbreak.

'No,' she uttered, wanting to bawl her eyes out. She was passing up on something so special. She would never love another man as she loved Andreo. But—

'You don't mean that.' Disregarding her uncoordinated attempts to put distance between them, Andreo cupped her face with gentle long-fingered hands, insisting that she met the silver warmth of his

eyes. 'I know you don't. I have never felt so drawn
to a woman as I am to you, and I've seen the hunger
in your eyes. I know how much you want me. I knew
it when you were in my bed; your response was more
than I had ever dreamed of. I bitterly regret that at
the time I felt I couldn't make it perfect for you in
my enfeebled state. When we make love it has to be
more than merely perfect.'

'Oh!' A stricken cry was wrenched from her and
her face flamed with embarrassed colour. He knew!
He'd known all the time! So much for his wicked
pretence that the events of that day were lost to him
in a fog of delirium!

Unavailingly attempting to twist away, Mercy
found herself captured by two strong arms, held
tightly against that lithe body as he sat back on one
of the chairs and pinioned her on his lap.

Resistance was futile; at least that was what Mercy
told herself as she felt her limbs go floppy, like a
wind-up toy with flat batteries.

She felt so very foolish. How he must have been
laughing at her! Knowing she had been not just responding but actively encouraging him! Then biding
his time, waiting until he judged the time was right.

One hand was on her waist, the other curving
around a too-generous hip. And that, to her mortification, was all she could concentrate on. Until he remarked conversationally, 'Physical desire is nothing
to be ashamed of. I never knew either of your parents,
of course. But which one taught you that sex is a sin?'

That, to her mind, was fighting talk! Her drooping-
with-shame head shot up. 'Neither! And don't you
dare suggest such a thing!'

Andreo grinned. His Mercy was the only woman ever to have the temerity to bawl him out—he had found her tendency to do just that remarkably refreshing right from the off. It had made him realise just how tedious it could be to have women fawning over him, simpering and agreeing with whatever opinion, no matter how outrageous, he came out with!

Sensing her intention to remove herself and stalk off in a huff, his hands tightened possessively as she lashed out at him, her lush, adorable breasts heaving with outrage. 'I was taught to respect my body. And I have no intention of being your housekeeper by day and your whore at night! And being—' her voice wavered, but she rallied magnificently '—being told to get lost as soon as you get bored.'

'You will never bore me,' he countered silkily, a teasing smile on his wilful mouth. 'And, as for respecting your body, so you should. Respect what it is telling you—that you and I were made for each other.' As if to hammer home that point, the hand that was curved around her hip slid down to her bottom to nudge her into contact with the hard proof of just how much she turned him on. 'Forget the housekeeper part—put it out of your mind.' The lightning realisation that no way did he want Mercy in a subservient position ever again hit him like a ton of bricks. He cleared his throat and continued thickly, 'I will hire a dozen cleaning ladies to follow your directions, allowing you to concentrate on being my woman, making me eat proper meals and stuffing my rooms with flowers and hanging chocolate box pictures on my dining room walls.'

Biting her tongue at that, Mercy had the good sense

to know when to stay silent. Privately she'd been amazed by his remarkable silence when she'd hung a print of a thatched cottage surrounded by millions of flowers amongst his collection of modern art because it reminded her of her home village and she couldn't make out what his paintings were meant to represent. But in the throes of turning to molten honey at the evidence of his arousal, she still retained enough sanity to point out—albeit with a shameful huskiness— 'I need to earn my living, in case you'd forgotten.'

One dark brow lifted lazily, his long mouth quirking with intense amusement as he countered, 'You would want for nothing, my angel. Beautiful clothes, fabulous sapphires to match your lovely eyes, diamonds fit for the purity of the heart of an angel and rubies for the privacy of our bedroom to match your passion and mine.'

Mercy clenched her teeth and swallowed a bubble of hysteria. A kept woman dripping with jewels didn't fit her idea of herself at all and she shouldn't give that demeaning picture houseroom in her head. She should put him straight immediately, tell him thanks but no thanks. She would housekeep for him because she had no option if she were to really help her brother, but he could forget the sex thing because all the jewels in the world could never heal a broken heart.

Knowing she had to spell it out and have him put her aside, put on his cold face and deprive her of what her feeble body clamoured for—this divine closeness to the man she loved—she battled with her emotions and tried to find the right words to convince him that she wasn't that sort of woman—the sort he was used to taking to his bed and turfing out of it the moment he got bored or a more exciting body entered his line of vision.

But something else was happening here. Something she had precious few defences against.

His hand was sliding beneath her skirt, resting lightly on her knee, then slowly sliding upwards. Mercy caught her breath, every cell in her body igniting as uncontrollable hunger had her fastening her dilated eyes on his utterly sensual mouth and dipping her head to claim it and her last semi-sane thought told her that she was going to regret this before dissolving in the white heat of his passionate response.

CHAPTER NINE

As THE morning heat beat around them from a cloud-less, sparkling blue sky Andreo rose to his feet with inherent fluid grace, effortlessly carrying Mercy, who clung on to him like a limpet, arms wrapped around his neck in a frenzy of raw lust, unable to resist claiming his too-tempting mouth with a thousand tiny kisses.

Striding back towards the villa like a man with a driven mission, Andreo suddenly paused, his large, lean and powerful body tensing as he stilled, sought her dazed eyes and held them with blazing silver intensity. He announced on a fractured, shockingly sexy breath, 'If we make it as far as my bed there will be no going back, my precious angel. Now is the time to say if you have any reservations.'

The entire length of Mercy's clinging body went rigid as deep shock claimed her when the import of his words penetrated her hitherto absent brain with the precision of a sharpened dagger.

Despite the blazing heat of the courtyard she felt cold right through to her bones and strangely giddy. What did she think she'd been doing? Compromising her high standards with wayward disregard for the consequences!

If he'd kept his so tempting, so beautiful mouth firmly shut, those words unsaid, she would have remained in her brain-numbing fog of acute physical hunger and continued to encourage him all the way! And the consequences of that folly would have meant hopeless heartbreak and an emptiness that would probably have remained with her for the rest of her life.

'I don't do sex without long-term commitment,' she at last pushed out squeakily, forcibly reminding herself more than she was laying down her rules to Andreo, the hands that had been lovingly feathering through the silky dark hair on the nape of his neck now thrusting against his chest. 'Please put me down.'

Noting the flare of frustration on his taut cheekbones as he slid her to her feet with a sudden and chillingly impersonal politeness, his magnificent eyes as bleak as charity, Mercy felt truly dreadful, cringingly ashamed of herself. She felt really horribly cheap. Didn't men have a nasty name for women who led them to the brink of no return and then backed off?

Despite all her self-protective instincts, the boringly repetitive lectures she'd delivered to herself, he only had to touch her to make her lose all sense and reason and offer herself on a plate!

She couldn't blame Andreo for grabbing what seemed to be so eagerly offered. By his own honest admission he had few moral qualms where women were concerned. He took what he wanted and discarded it as soon as the novelty wore off. She knew that. Yet still she had been with him every inch of the way, all greedy hands and lips!

This huge mess was all her own fault!

About to tender her sincere apologies, grovel if need be, beg him to try to understand her point of view and not hate her too much, the words were stopped in her throat as a female voice calling his name sliced through the hot silent air of the courtyard.

'*Madre.*'

His tone very formal, eyes a flinty grey, the usual light of vitality absent, Andreo stepped past Mercy after a long moment of absolute stillness, heading with no great show of eagerness towards the slight yet commanding figure standing in the arched doorway that accessed the courtyard from the front of the villa.

What bad timing! Mercy agonised. Her dearly loved Andreo had just been showered with a metaphorical bucket of icy water by a woman who had been a squirming bundle of avid need in his arms only moments ago. And in the immediate aftermath a woman he had greeted as his mother had walked in on him. Her whole body ached for him!

Her eyes on stalks, her heart thumping, Mercy watched as he lifted the elderly woman's hand and air-kissed the fingers before asking drily, 'And to what do I owe this pleasure?'

'As I've heard nothing from you since that brief phone call last Christmas, and could raise no response from your London home or the Rome apartment, I phoned Sonniva's mobile and found that she was on leave.'

The other woman's expressionless light grey eyes swept to Mercy, pinning her to the spot as she wondered sickly how much of that earlier torrid scene Andreo's formidable mother had silently witnessed. All of it, judging by the look of displeasure on that coldly arrogant face!

A displeasure also directed at her son, Mercy decided as the elderly woman censured, 'Puzzled by her unscheduled leave, Sonniva had quite rightly made discreet enquiries and discovered that you were here. With a woman.'

A flicker of perplexity crossed her autocratic features as she regarded Mercy's red with embarrassment skin. 'Won't you introduce us?'

No mention of her housekeeperly status, Mercy noted as Andreo coolly obliged. Perhaps, she reasoned, he knew his stiff and, judging by the look of her, not likely to unbend parent would be horrified if she knew he had been cavorting with a mere servant!

Stepping further into the courtyard, Signora Pascali suddenly halted, put a hand to her grey silk-clad chest and swayed on her feet, her face turning an alarming ashen, her breathing rapid and shallow. Immediately, Andreo was at her side, a supportive hand tucked beneath her elbow. 'You have overtired yourself in this heat, Mamma. Come, sit.'

'It is nothing.' Tersely speaking as she jerked her arm from her son's supportive hand, she progressed with slow dignity towards the group of chairs around the table. 'I had my chauffeur drive me because I wanted to tell you in person that in one week's time I am to have heart surgery. They are to fit a pacemaker. I thought that you, as my only kin, should know this.'

Andreo had visibly paled as he drew a chair further into the shade of the arbour and saw his mother seated. 'Is it serious?' he demanded. 'Why have you not told me you were unwell before this?'

'Would you have found time in your rackety life to have been remotely interested?'

Andreo drew a hiss of breath between his teeth, ignoring that slur as he stated, 'You will give me the name of your consultant and I will speak to him about your condition, as is my right.'

Mercy slipped silently back into the villa. What had passed between mother and son had shaken her rigid. She knew next to nothing about Andreo's family— only that his father had died many years ago and that his grandfather had given him really cynical advice. Recalling how close she had always been to both her parents, she couldn't find it in herself to understand why those two appeared to be at daggers drawn.

But she did know that the kind of barely veiled sniping that had passed for conversation between mother and son couldn't be good for a plainly unwell woman.

Taking a bottle of spring water from the cavernous fridge in the farmhouse-style kitchen, she filled a tall glass, added ice cubes and hurried back to the courtyard. Signora Pascali didn't need to waste her energy on coming out with spiky comments, she needed a bit of TLC, whether she wanted it or not.

'Sip at this, it will help you to feel cooler.' She put the glass into the thin, long-boned hands, her voice gentle. 'You're looking much better already. Your colour's come back,' Mercy then offered bracingly, a firm believer in being optimistic around the sick and infirm because doom and gloom would only make the sufferer feel worse. And earned herself an arched eyebrow of surprise and a distant, *'Grazie.'*

'My mother will be staying overnight,' Andreo announced with the look of a man who had won a monumental victory, swinging on his heel and imparting, 'Lucca, her chauffeur, will stay with Sonniva. I will arrange it.'

Leaving Mercy to take a seat opposite the *signora*. 'I'll make a room ready for you, and then you can rest. Have you had to come far?'

'A hundred kilometres.'

About eighty miles? Mercy endeavoured to translate, disregarding the frigid delivery of that information. 'Then taking a break before you return home is common sense. It was very kind of you to make the effort to come in person to break the news to Andreo—it will mean a lot to him—when you could have picked up the phone once you'd found out where he was.'

Warming to her subject, ignoring the decidedly prickly atmosphere, because mother and son were obviously at cross purposes over something or other and the spiky elderly woman must, deep down, be very fond of her son or she wouldn't have come all this way to see him, she imparted, 'It's natural to turn to loved ones in time of trouble or stress. And you'll be very apprehensive.' Probably wondering if she'd survive the operation, which would account for her wanting to see her son and break the news in person, poor thing! 'You wouldn't be human if you weren't a little bit worried. But I've heard that the success rate of that particular operation is very high, and it's marvellous what modern surgery can achieve.'

'I see my housekeeper is doing her Angel of Mercy thing,' Andreo mused from behind her. 'I have discovered she is very good at it. From personal experience.'

Did he have to remind her? Mercy could have smacked him for the snide reminder of the way she'd behaved when he'd first been ill. And now the fat was truly in the fire! His aristocratic parent would blow a gasket if she learned that her son had been getting up close and very intimate with a mere hireling.

Not that she would have lied about her position to the older woman, but it would have been better for his mother's peace of mind if nothing had been said. Why did he have to put his foot in it?

Glancing over her shoulder to where he stood, butter wouldn't melt, she met his charismatic smile and looked quickly back again, hot and flustered, tummy looping crazily, stumbling to her feet and announcing unsteadily, 'I will make a room ready, *signora*, and then a little light lunch.'

And escaped.

The room she had chosen to make ready for Signora Pascali's occupation looked out over the paved courtyard and the gauzy curtains fluttered at the tall open windows, admitting a welcome herb-scented breeze.

She'd made the bed up with crisp lavender-scented sheets, put fresh towels and soap in the *en suite* bathroom and placed a carafe of iced water beside a crystal glass on the night table.

Unable to find an excuse to linger any longer than she already had, Mercy left the room and headed downstairs with deep trepidation. Her insides still squirmed with embarrassment and shame whenever she recalled what had happened earlier that morning, how hotly she'd responded to Andreo—led him on and then backed off, protesting squeakily like a prim Victorian virgin—he would have decided with deep contempt. He must be thinking very badly of her.

And that his aristocratic parent should have arrived to witness a torrid scene between her wealthy, top-of-his-field, handsome son and a mere servant made her feel very uncomfortable indeed. Had Signora Pascali labelled her as an unprincipled gold-digger, a member of the lower orders out to take her wealthy employer for everything she could get her grubby hands on?

Recognising that she was being paranoid because nobody in the twenty-first century could possibly be that snobbish, or she devoutly hoped not, Mercy straightened her spine and marched into the big airy kitchen and began to make a cold salmon salad, making sure the air conditioning was working in the elegant dining room and laying two place settings, taking her time over it.

She would eat in the kitchen and leave mother and son to talk in privacy and, hopefully, embark on a conversation that was less spiky than the initial one had been.

Pinning a carefully arranged serene smile on her face and hoping that the Pascalis weren't still verbally tearing strips off each other, Mercy, heart bumping against her ribs, finally walked out into the courtyard to announce that lunch was ready and found it empty of human occupation.

She was horribly disconcerted by the sudden sense of loss. Could she have actually been looking forward to feasting her eyes on Andreo's drop-dead-gorgeous person, revelling in his powerfully raw sexuality? If so she was a nut case, in serious trouble!

After this morning's debacle he would want nothing more to do with her, and she couldn't blame him. She wasn't the sort of raving beauty who would get under a man's skin—especially the love 'em and leave 'em type that Andreo had cheerfully admitted to being.

He would go back to calling her Howard, would do his best to ignore her while keeping his eyes peeled for her replacement.

And it was all her own fault! Mortified by her own inability to keep a lid on things, she set about running mother and son to earth, heading for the coolness of the inner sitting room.

Andreo would have taken his mother there, out of the heat. She had seen how he had immediately rushed to offer her his support when she had seemed about to faint, how he had paled when she'd told him of her coming heart operation. She'd also noted how Signora Pascali had brushed his hand aside as if she couldn't bear any support coming from his direction.

Despite the coldness of his initial greeting when his parent had first so unexpectedly appeared—and Mercy simply had to put that down to the highly emotional scene she had just interrupted and his state of savage frustration—he had been deeply concerned when he'd learned of the coming operation and the repudiation of his caring must have really hurt him.

Mercy's loving heart twisted painfully for him as she entered the arched doorway into the elegance of the hazy blue and cream sitting room and found only Signora Pascali in occupation, perched stiffly on one of the blue and soft gold brocade-covered wing-chairs.

Suffering a sudden fierce dislike of this rigid, cold woman who showed no maternal love for the man she herself adored, her fixed smile making her face ache, she imparted as pleasantly as she was able, 'I've put a cold lunch in the dining room. I must tell Signor Pascali. Can you tell me where I can find him?'

The older woman rose to her feet, the grey silk skirt of her beautifully crafted dress falling in elegant folds around her legs. 'Under the circumstances there is no need for you to refer to my son in the formal manner.'

Cringingly aware of the 'circumstances', Mercy felt her face redden and suffered the slightly amused assessment of a pair of grey eyes, so like her son's but lacking that spark of devilish vitality.

'Andreo is not here; he insisted on phoning my consultant and he further insisted he drive immediately to Naples to interview him on the subject of my condition. *Ohimé!* He is always ridiculously impetuous! Headstrong and inconsiderate since the day he was born! Give me your arm. You and I will lunch together, otherwise I shall find myself abandoned.'

Mercy pinkened with outrage. Rather than lunch with this woman she would prefer to throw her right out of the door! But, mindful of her heart condition, she offered the support of her arm as instructed and contented herself with a cool, '*Signora*, I don't think his actions show a lack of consideration. Insisting on personally checking on your state of health, that is. It shows he cares. And it's in his creative nature to be impetuous.'

'You rush to defend him. That is good!' At her

side, the older woman vented a tiny chuckle. 'And please, call me Claudia,' she insisted, pronouncing it Cloudier. 'I must say,' she stated as they entered the dining room, 'that salad looks quite delicious. My son tells me you are the best housekeeper he could hope to have.'

As Andreo's formidable mother took her seat at the table, Mercy passed her the serving spoons and the crystal bowl in which she'd assembled the pieces of cold salmon, prawns, sliced avocado and baby tomatoes on a bed of dressed green leaves and decided, from the high praise he had apparently handed out, that he had no burning intention to get rid of her services at the first opportunity that presented itself, in spite of what had happened earlier that morning.

And that wasn't the best of news.

She knew it would hurt unbearably if he told her that her services as housekeeper were no longer required and she were never to see him again, but that would be definitely easier to handle than if she stayed around him and she inevitably—given her track record in that direction—gave in to what her feeble body so ardently craved only to come up against his self-admitted low boredom threshold and find herself dumped.

She loved him but he wasn't for her, so she should have the strength of character to walk away the exact second they landed back in England, never set eyes on him again and save herself a barrow load of broken-hearted grief in the future. The loss of her highly paid job would be a blow to James, but for the first time in her life she should put her own well-being at the top of the list.

'In the short time before he left for Naples my son told me all about you. At my insistence.' The *signora*'s cool voice broke into Mercy's troubled thoughts. 'At this late stage I have discovered that my ill health has the power to draw confidences from my close-lipped offspring.'

'All?' With great care Mercy laid her fork back on the porcelain plate. What, exactly, had he said?

'Oh, I doubt it.' Claudia speared a prawn and actually smiled. 'But enough about your background, your personality, to persuade me you are far different from the usual creatures he takes to his bed. Oh—' she waved a thin hand expressively '—I have never actually met one of them—and never had the slightest wish to—but I have seen pictures of them with him in the press, read reports in the gossip columns. Reports I always tried to keep hidden from his father. Poor Aldo was so disappointed in his only child, I did not want to make matters worse. As for me, I prayed nightly that Andreo would meet a caring, sensible woman who would domesticate him, marry him and put an end to his wild ways.'

Mercy choked back a hysterical giggle. No sane woman would ever want to domesticate him, change him. Any woman who loved him would revel in his volatility, his vitality, his massive untidiness and extravagant nature. But Andreo had no interest in marriage—not in the forseeable future—and that sobering thought chased away any inclination to giggle, making her wish she hadn't eaten her lunch because she suddenly felt queasy.

Unaware of her companion's tumultuous emotions, Claudia laid down her own fork and dabbed her lips delicately with her linen napkin. 'At last I have hopes that my son is learning sense. You are a decent woman. You blush easily, which speaks of a sensitive nature, unused to devious dealings, you cook beautifully, so I'm told—and lunch was superb—you do not have money or social standing, but that is nothing set against your admirable upbringing as the daughter of a country clergyman and your domestic talents and your good common sense—yes—' she arched a finely drawn brow '—I am told that you even tried to curb his household extravagances. But for now I will hold my tongue and keep my hopes high. And perhaps you will show me to the room where I am to rest.'

Complying, Mercy had to force back the words that would disabuse Andreo's mother. He had no intention of marrying, and when he eventually did it wouldn't be to someone like her. When he finally bit the bullet and decided he needed an heir he would only tie the knot with someone who had masses of money in her own right and it wouldn't matter if she had a face like a dustbin!

Let the poor woman keep her illusions—her hopes—until she'd recovered from her operation and was in a fit state to understand that those maternal hopes had been very foolish. Holding her tongue on that subject was the only charitable thing to do.

But as she opened the door to the room she had made ready she couldn't help pointing out, 'Andreo isn't hopeless. He's widely respected, and not only in his chosen field. And I think you're fonder of him than you like to show. If you weren't you wouldn't have put yourself to the trouble of coming here today.

I think you should try to show your fondness more,
enjoy him for who and what he is. And be proud
of him.'

Looking after Claudia Pascali was like caring for a
cross between a self-willed child and a royal personage, Mercy decided as she flopped into an armchair
in the sitting room later that evening to wait for
Andreo's return.

To take her mind off the giant flock of butterflies
in her tummy, engendered by her need to apologise
for her inexcusable behaviour this morning and not
knowing quite how to go about it without making him
even more disgusted with her than he already was,
she mentally replayed the trials and tribulations of her
day.

After a remarkably short afternoon nap Claudia had
descended and run her to earth watering the pots of
herbs in the courtyard and demanded the use of the
phone, a sheet of paper and a pen.

'My chauffeur will be here in ten minutes to drive
you into town. I have written a list of the items I need.
Not expecting to stay overnight, I am not prepared.'

With the list in her hand, Mercy had battled
through the crowds and the afternoon heat to track
down the amazing amount of overnight necessities,
all precisely detailed, and had returned to a demand
for freshly squeezed orange juice followed by her as-
sistance in a short stroll around the grounds.

It had been just an excuse for something that re-
sembled the Spanish Inquisition, Mercy remembered.
But she had answered as honestly as she could, airing
details of her background and that of both parents,
her sketchy knowledge of both sets of grandparents,

her views of the permissive society, her desire to have children.

Then there had been the question of what to have for supper, which would be taken at the long, sturdy table in the kitchen as she, Claudia Pascali, did not believe in standing on ceremony.

Not half! Mercy had thought inelegantly as her charge had mused her way through a long list of options, eventually settling on a simple herb omelette and green salad, to be followed by a little diced fresh fruit.

The very moment the omelette had been produced—light, fluffy and golden—Claudia had announced, 'I am rather more tired than I expected. I will not wait for Andreo's return; it was his idea to go chasing off, not mine. I'll speak again to him in the morning before I leave.' Rising from the chair where she had been assessing Mercy's every movement with the eagle eye of an examiner, she demanded, 'Bring a tray to my room in half an hour. I will unpack the items you brought for me and have an early night.'

In half an hour the omelette would be like leather! Another must be prepared and ready in half an hour on the dot!

The elderly lady was more like her son than she would care to acknowledge, Mercy thought as she carried up the tray at the prescribed time to be greeted by a sea of discarded wrappers, paper bags, tissue paper and carriers and the information that the night-dress would do nicely but the sleeves of the dressing robe were too long, the bristles of the toothbrush too hard but the night cream was exactly right.

And now, feeling frazzled, Mercy waited, getting more uptight by the second, her eyes continually straying to the small but ornate ormulu mantel-clock.

What could she possibly say to him that would put things back to the way they had been, with her as a useful servant in the background of his life?

And if she found the magic formula, what then?

In all probability Andreo would readily slip back into the status quo, shrug those fantastic shoulders and write her off as a tease or a prude, a dead loss when it came to sexual games. Forget he had ever— if only fleetingly—fancied her and, in his own time, crook his finger in the direction of a sexy female who knew the score and didn't bleat about the long-term commitments he had no intention of making.

And what of her? Could she continue to work for him, see him every day, loving him, needing him?

Her nerves felt hot-wired. In an attempt to distract herself, she sprang to her feet and fled to the kitchen to wash the floor.

She was on her hands and knees when the blackness beyond the kitchen windows was banished by a flood of soft amber light, an indication that someone had triggered the security lights.

Andreo?

Her stomach leapt up to her throat in choking panic, then plummeted sickeningly down to the soles of her feet.

How on earth was she going to handle this?

CHAPTER TEN

TELL the truth and shame the devil?

It was a maxim that had been firmly instilled into her since birth.

Come clean and confess that she'd fallen deeply in love with him but was too cowardly to put herself forward as a contender for the title of The Heartbreak Queen of the Decade!

Impossible!

Flushed and flustered, her heart bumping, Mercy hauled the bucket of hot soapy water to empty it down the outside drain, get rid of the evidence of her inability to relax, and ran headlong into Andreo.

The capable hands that steadied her felt like fire on her flesh but she knew they had to be impersonal because his features were bleaker than she'd ever seen them.

Tell him the truth and he'd, quite rightly, call her a fool, laugh like a drain.

But he didn't look capable of laughing at anything as he disposed of the contents of the bucket and dropped it with a clatter, striding past her into the kitchen and heading for one of the cupboards.

Extracting a bottle of brandy, he dumped a couple of inches into a glass and tipped the bottle towards her. 'Join me?'

Mercy shook her head wordlessly. Drink strong liquor and she'd lose what few wits remained to her.

'Then bear with me, keep me company. I take it my mother has retired for the night?' He didn't wait for her answer. 'I don't want to be alone.'

His eyes looked haunted, his features strained. Replacing the bottle, he carried his drink through to the sitting room and, after a moment of dithering hesitation, Mercy followed.

He wanted her to keep him company, stick around. Which had to mean that he wasn't still mad at her for the way she'd back-pedalled this morning. She wouldn't have to answer any awkward questions or listen to him calling her a tease, or worse. Which was what she'd expected as soon as he'd got her alone and was free to lash her with scorn. Though, loving him, she badly wanted to apologise for her behaviour.

Then she mentally spouted a string of bad words, the sort that would have her parents turning in their graves.

How could she be so all-fired self-centred? This wasn't about her at all! How big-headed could she get?

He'd probably forgotten all about the episode that made her feel ill with embarrassment, shame and contrition every time she thought about it. He'd have written it off as an unimportant non-event, put her firmly back in the slot she'd been hired to fill—a servant to cater to his every whim, put up with his every mood. It was concern for his parent that was occupying his mind to the exclusion of all else. He only wanted her around in her servile capacity, to fetch and carry for him, maybe fix him something to eat.

He was sitting at the end of one of the two matching cream-upholstered sofas, his glossy head downbent, the empty glass loosely clasped in one hand. She had never imagined the super-confident, vital Andreo Pascali could look so vulnerable.

Mercy's eyes darkened with concern, her soft, loving heart going straight out to him. She longed to wrap comforting arms around him, beg him not to worry, but guessed that he wouldn't welcome physical contact coming from her direction.

Instead she sat beside him, careful not to get too close and enquired gently, 'You saw your mother's consultant; is the prognosis good?' And held her breath in case it wasn't and she'd said the wrong thing, because if it was good he surely wouldn't be looking so drained and beaten.

He angled a glimmering sideways look at her, a lock of dark hair falling over one strongly marked brow. Mercy's fingers itched to smooth it back into place so she bunched her hands into fists on her lap to make good and sure she couldn't.

'Apparently, yes, it is good. But there is always a slight risk.'

'Well, I shouldn't dwell on that, if I were you,' Mercy soothed. 'Try to think positively.'

'But I'm not you, am I?' Andreo pointed out on a harsh bite, his head snapping up, silver eyes glittering with sudden, shrivelling scorn. 'I'm not a little ray of sunshine, neither am I a perfect goody-two-shoes! I bet you were the apple of your parents' eyes and never gave them a moment's worry!'

He slumped back against the sofa cushions, his eyes closed as if his outburst had robbed him of all energy, and intoned on a flattened sigh, 'You don't know what you're talking about.'

A frown knotted Mercy's smooth brow. He was obviously deeply troubled. She couldn't imagine what that outburst had been about. Tentatively, she suggested, 'Then enlighten me.'

On a typical burst of relentless energy, he shot upright again and raked his fingers through his already rumpled hair and ground out on a burst of savage frustration, 'Enlighten you? That would take some doing!'

His narrowed eyes speared the wide blue innocence of hers, the soft and gentle curve of her lovely lips. His own mouth compressed, he threw at her, 'Could you possibly understand how it feels to have been a disappointment to your parents practically from the moment you learned to walk and talk? My father died before I could earn his approval for a single thing about me or the way I choose to live my life. It was a shock to learn that my mother—whom I adore— might do the same! Satisfied?'

'I don't understand,' Mercy said uncertainly, instinctively covering one of his hands with hers because he was hurting. 'Why should anyone be disappointed in you? If you were my son I'd be really proud of you.'

Which earned her the shock of an unexpected slow smile and an enigmatic, 'If I were your son I'd feel cheated.' The hand that had lain still beneath hers now moved to twine their fingers together, leaving her in no doubt about what he'd meant. Her heart flipped and her mind went into freefall, unable to get to grips with his sudden mood changes. Why was he back to teasing, flirting just a little? After this morning it made no kind of sense.

Gazing into her bewildered eyes, he confessed fracturedly, 'I'm sorry. I have no right to take my guilt out on you.' His fingers tightened on hers as he told her, 'My father was a lawyer of great repute. Came from a long line of them. Sober, industrious, astute. Dry. It was forcibly impressed on me that I was supposed to follow in the illustrious footsteps of my revered ancestors. But I had other ideas.' He shrugged fatalistically. 'I knew what I wanted to do, and went straight ahead and did it—'

'And made a huge success of it,' Mercy assured him, pulling herself together with an effort and wondering how any parent could be so controlling and not be happy to allow a child to follow his own star. 'Surely they could see that?'

He shook his head in denial. 'All either of them could see was my lifestyle. I drove fast cars and dated unsuitable women and followed what they termed a rackety, vulgar career. I should be doing something solid—and boring!—settling down and raising a family! I know the lectures by heart, which is why, over the years I saw less and less of them.' His features tightened with bitter regret. 'I could have tried harder to make them understand that by rejecting the type of life they had mapped out for me I wasn't rejecting them.'

Inwardly Mercy was furious with his parents for heaping this unnecessary guilt on him but her need to comfort him was stronger than any desire to put her anger at what they had done into words.

Her free hand lifted to lie against the taut set of his prominent cheekbone and the starkly carved hollow beneath as she consoled gently, 'There is still time.

Truly there is. Not only after the operation when your mother will be as good as new, but before. She's very fond of you—she wouldn't have wanted to see you, break her news in person, if she weren't. She might not be very good at showing it—some people aren't—but mother love is stronger than all that tradition stuff. You just need to open up, tell her what you told me—about not rejecting them along with their views.'

'You would make a perfect mother.' Disconcertingly, he took her meant-to-be-soothing hand and pressed kisses into her palm and Mercy, her power to breathe deserting her, said huskily, 'Don't go there...'

'No?' One dark brow arched over his stunning eyes as his mouth found her inner wrist where her pulse had jumped to frantic, leaping life. Held by his magnetic silver eyes, Mercy couldn't speak. But her mind was racing, loving him to bits as she reasoned that what he needed was genuine warmth and caring.

Brought up by harsh, disapproving parents, given cynical advice by his grandfather, he had never experienced any outward show of unstinting love so didn't know how to give it.

Impulsively, a lump in her throat, she leant closer and planted a kiss on the top of his downbent head. It was meant to be a there-there gesture, the sort anyone would give to a troubled soul, but his reaction turned it into something completely other.

His head came up, his arms sweeping her into the hard curve of his body and capturing her there as his mouth claimed hers with a driven hunger that was vocalised by the purring groan deep in his throat.

Mercy trembled violently, her bones melting as she

instinctively, and without a rational argument in her head, met and answered his explosive passion.

This one man, the man she loved, needed the warmth of human contact, craved it, and how could she deny him when she adored him now and always? Her future didn't matter; she had stopped thinking like a selfish wimp and scuttling away at the first sign of danger. He needed her, she needed him, needed to be truly generous and show him all the love she was capable of giving.

Joy blossomed inside her, welling up like molten lava and filling her with certainty as her arms, her mouth, her whole body clung to him. Her eyes misted over as she dragged her lips from the fiery passion of his and whispered, her voice slurred with urgency, 'Make love to me, Andreo,'

She felt his lean, rangy body go very still before he dragged a breath deep into his lungs, buried his face into the curve of her neck, his lips slow and sweet against her sensitised skin as he uttered, 'I ache for you, my sweet angel! How I ache!'

His hands deftly parted the silky fabric at her neckline, exposing her breasts, and she slid back against the cushions, her spine arching in ecstasy as his dark head bent to take one engorged nipple into his mouth and then the other.

Writhing beneath him, intoxicated and incandescent, Mercy was barely aware of being scooped up into strong, determined arms, being carried, being lain on his bed, only knew that her arms were clinging, reluctant to have contact broken as he straightened.

'Patience, my angel.' His sensual mouth quirked in the slightest smile, his eyes darkening to the softest charcoal, smouldering between the narrowing effect of sultrily lowered dense sable lashes. His hands, not too steady, she noticed, undid shirt buttons. Slowly. 'I have dreamed of this moment for so long. It must not be rushed as if we were callow teenagers.' The shirt drifted to the floor. 'What we are about to share will be exquisite.'

Mercy's dazed eyes fought to focus on his naked torso, desperate to imprint the perfection of the taut muscles, the smooth bronzed skin, on her memory banks so that in future she could access them and recapture this stolen time, remember the breathtaking beauty of giving all she was, unstintingly and with joy, to the only man she would ever love.

His long fingers were at the waistband of the superbly tailored narrow grey trousers he'd worn for his appointment with the consultant, hesitating then dropping away as he turned to bend over her, his breathing shallow and ragged as he stripped away her top, his hands sliding urgently over the lush ripeness of her breasts, down to her engagingly tiny waist and the unwanted barrier of her full skirt.

Aiding and abetting, Mercy arched her hips to make the disposal of the garment as easy as possible and waited, breath stilled, heart crashing, as he slid her tiny white briefs down the length of her legs.

Her breath sobbing in her lungs, Mercy squirmed with almost intolerable pleasure as he locked his eyes with hers and ran his fingers along one slender, quivering thigh and found the moist, pulsating heat of her desire, making her cry out with frantic excitement, her whole being on fire, concentrated on a sensation so intense she thought she might die of it.

Instead, he sat beside her, gathered her up and rocked her in his arms, his soft clean breath feathering the side of her face as he murmured, 'Slowly, my sweet angel. We have all the time in the world. Trust me in this. It shall be perfect for you. I shall give you such pleasure. You shall never forget, I promise.'

Of course she would never forget. How could one forget perfection?

As she had expected, Mercy woke alone. She viewed the vastly disarranged bed with sombre eyes and ran a tentative finger over kiss-swollen lips.

She had no regrets, not a single one, she reminded herself staunchly. She had made love with Andreo because she adored him and he had needed her and now she had a memory that would remain with her, treasured, for the rest of her life.

He had made love to her because he'd needed the comfort of a woman's body and she'd been there, and willing. More than. And soon she'd be as forgotten as all the others. Sex, fantastic sex, was for him a substitute for the love he couldn't give.

She knew that. Had accepted it. She would not get all clingy and moony-eyed, a supplicant for the love he didn't have to give.

Yet her heart performed an acrobatic flip as he walked into the room. Unabashed male perfection. A lock of dark hair falling over his forehead, he was dressed this morning in a dark blue sleeveless shirt open at the neck and hip-hugging blue denims.

Mercy swallowed rapidly, hating the way her mouth had gone so dry. 'I was just about to get up. How late is it?' she asked, doing her best to sound nonchalant, wondering if she was coming over as the type of woman who viewed last night's events as no big deal, with no inclination to cling, expect more than he was prepared to give.

'In your own time, no mad hurry.' His feet were planted slightly apart, his hands in the pockets of his jeans, pulling the worn fabric tight across his pelvis, his eyes thoughtful as he imparted, 'There's something I didn't tell you last night. Following my interview with my mother's consultant, her operation's been rescheduled for the day after tomorrow, so that I can use my time here in Italy to be with her. Lucca shall drive her home this morning—she doesn't trust my driving.'

He permitted himself a wry smile. 'So I shall follow, be with her until she is recovered, at home and with a professional nurse for the period of her recuperation. I told her of the new arrangements just now when I took a breakfast tray to her.'

Dismay flooded through her with a rush that made her feel slightly nauseous. He would be leaving soon. So soon that there would be no place for her within the vigil he meant to keep.

Then she felt really sick, sick at herself. Such were the maundering thoughts she'd promised herself she would not entertain. She shot into a sitting position among the heaped pillows. Then, remembering her nakedness, she tugged a sheet up to her chin in misplaced belated modesty.

'How did she take it?' she questioned, hoping the elderly woman wasn't too fazed by the bringing forward of an operation she was probably dreading, carefully ignoring the humorous upward drift of one black brow at her scramble for decency.

'Very well. And Mercy, I'll speak to her, as you suggested I should.' His voice softened. 'Thank you. I didn't get the chance to make my peace with my father. It is important that I don't make the same mistake again. Even if she comes out with all the same lectures, I'll know I did try.'

'I'm sure she won't!' Mercy sounded hearteningly positive but beneath the sheet her fingers were tightly crossed. Surely his mother would finally see things from Andreo's point of view, understand that a round peg couldn't be forced into a square hole, and be proud that her son was such a high achiever.

For a heart-lurching moment Mercy thought he was about to come to her but she saw him stay the slight forward movement, stiffen his shoulders, as he told her flatly, 'Sonniva, my housekeeper, will arrive within the hour. Later, her husband Gianni will drive you to the airport for the early evening flight back to London. I've arranged for your ticket to be waiting at check-in.' He shot a troubled glance at the face of his wafer-thin gold wrist-watch. 'I should be back in London with you in around a fortnight and then we can have a long overdue talk.'

About what? she asked herself dully as she watched him exit. According to him, he always laid down the rules at the start of an affair. No strings, no recriminations. She didn't want to hear that.

Last night had been a once in a lifetime night of magic. A precious magical night she would never forget. She couldn't bear it to be sullied by listening to him lay down his cynical ground rules.

Forcing herself out of bed, she headed for the *en suite* bathroom, collecting yesterday's clothes on the way.

In two weeks he would be back at his London home.

But she would be long gone.

It was the only way.

CHAPTER ELEVEN

ANDREO strode out of the private clinic, his mood buoyant. Claudia's operation had gone well and she'd come through the critical post-op recovery period with flying colours. Her surgeon promised a full recovery with many good years ahead of her and the weight he'd felt lift from his shoulders allowed him to breathe at last.

As he covered the short distance to the hotel he was using here in Naples to be near the clinic he felt as if he were walking on air, the release of tension leaving him light-headed. Tonight he would sleep for the first time in more than forty-eight hours.

The hot early evening air was alive with the ubiquitous sounds of traffic and raucous humanity and it was with deep relief that he entered the hush of his air-conditioned suite, ordered grilled prawns, black coffee and wine from room service, stripped off his clothes and headed for the shower.

Tomorrow morning he would sit with Claudia for an hour or two, enjoy the knowledge that she would make a full recovery and build on the new closeness that had followed their discussion on the evening before she'd been admitted to the clinic.

Then, while she rested, he would drive out to the sedate Chiaia neighbourhood where his mother, retiring to the city of her birth after the death of his father, had bought a small villa. There he would speak with

Maria, Claudia's companion, and the rest of her staff and let them know that an agency nurse would be in residence to make sure Claudia did nothing to tire herself for the period of her convalescence when she was discharged from the clinic because he would have to return to London and wouldn't be around to make sure she took things easily.

Twenty minutes later, Andreo gave up on the prawns and poured a second glass of wine.

The tension was back.

Mercy.

He'd hated having to leave everything unresolved between them but under the fraught circumstances, the change of plans, he'd had no choice.

Surely she would understand?

His angel was the most understanding human being he had ever known. Truly beautiful, inside and out.

His heart squeezed painfully inside his breast. There was so much he had to say to her. There had been no time during those final few hours. An atmosphere of controlled rush and bustle, the need to appear calm and optimistic for his mother's sake, hadn't been conducive to gentle persuasion.

He knew what was needed. Candlelight, soft music, fine wine, romancing and touching. Lots of touching. He knew how her breath caught when he touched her, her glorious eyes hazing over with the mists of desire.

He groaned, slammed his glass down on the table, stuck his fisted hands into the pockets of the towelling robe he wore and paced the room.

Madre di Dio! When he thought of their night together, of the beauty of her nakedness, the way she had reached for him, clung, her gloriously sexy mouth responding to his passion with such magnificent generosity, he thought he would explode with impatience.

He missed her desperately. He needed to be with her. Wanted to be with her. But for now that simply wasn't possible.

He should have insisted she stay on in Italy with him. He cursed himself violently for not thinking of it.

But he could phone her. Speak to her.

Now.

His hand hovered over his mobile, then dropped back to his side.

He could say—what?

That he loved her.

She wouldn't believe him. She knew his track record, his views on commitment. She'd heard it all from his own big mouth!

He needed to show her, needed time to convince her that he had changed, needed time stretching way into infinity if necessary, time to seduce her, over and over, until she did believe him. Until she understood that she couldn't live without him.

Practically incandescent with frustration, he took himself off to bed. An early night to catch up on lost sleep. Like a sensible man. Trouble was, he didn't feel sensible.

Dio! Never long on patience, he was going to have to learn it. And fast.

Thumping the switch that deactivated the superfluity of up-and-down lighters, spots and an ultra-modern overhead contraption, he stared into the darkness.

And saw her face.

Earnest and cute, surrounded by all those crinkly wild curls, exhorting him to eat a proper breakfast, her body covered in the huge, shapeless thing she used to wear around his home, making her look like a large bundle of washing, giving not the smallest hint of the fantastic curves hidden beneath.

The captivating smile that never failed to make his heart beat faster until he felt he was drowning in the bewitching radiance of it. The hurt darkening those astonishingly blue eyes when she'd accused him of hiring her for that ad because she was fat and ugly.

The faint rose-tinged flush of pleasure when he'd explained that she was not ugly, that she was the type of woman a real man would prefer over any amount of glossily packaged bimbos. He'd meant it too. Unreservedly. Though, stupidly, he hadn't recognised the significance of that at the time.

It had taken the shock of her transformation to do that. He had immediately wanted to bed her. And it had taken more time still—crass fool that he was!—to make him understand that he wanted, needed, very much more. For the first time in his life he had found the one woman he could love, could spend his whole life with, faithful until the end.

But did his Mercy want what he wanted?

He punched the pillow until it fell to the floor. Sleep! How could he expect himself to sleep when his mind was in turmoil?

Venting a bad-tempered sigh, he told himself that she had to want what he did—total commitment. There was no point in beating himself up, was there? Not when the way she'd responded to his love-making pointed that way. His angel wasn't the type of woman who would have an affair without turning a hair, for what she hoped to get out of him, the type of woman who had passed through his life in the past without leaving a ripple.

She was a well brought up vicar's daughter, for pity's sake!

Hadn't she, on that fatal morning, called a halt, telling him that she didn't do sex without long-term commitment? And he, instead of feeling furious and frustrated, had felt a huge wave of tenderness, reverence even, flood right through him, following on the revealing self-knowledge that he too wanted that long-term commitment. More than he'd ever wanted anything. He would have told her that but Claudia's arrival, her disturbing news, had put paid to that.

His brow smoothed, then almost immediately furrowed again as he recalled that later, on the evening of that same day, the highly moral scruples she had claimed had been nowhere in sight! She had actually begged him to make love to her! So what did that tell him?

He had never felt unsure of himself in the whole of his life.

He did now and he didn't like it!

He couldn't stand not knowing. He couldn't wait patiently around like a stuffed shirt until Claudia was released from the clinic and he was free to return to London.

Forget the long game—soft music and champagne—the slow, gently seductive approach!

Thumping the switch, he winced as enough lights to illuminate a fairground sprang to life and picked up his mobile.

She would sleep tonight, Mercy decided with forced optimism as she rinsed her solitary teacup under the tap at the kitchen sink.

Today, her third day back in London, she had actually managed to pull herself out of the unwanted, unnecessary fog of misery that had descended on her when she'd watched Andreo lovingly settle his mother into the back of her chauffeur-driven limo. She had then turned back to the villa, where Sonniva was minutely inspecting her kitchen for any mess or damage that might have occurred during her short absence.

She hadn't been able to watch her darling Andreo drive away, knowing she would never see him again.

Today she had been busy, busy, because she'd gritted her teeth and forced herself to stop mooning around and feeling doomy. Had made herself do something positive. Booking herself into a cheap hostel, signing on at the domestic agency because the money she had saved and earned from filming had been paid into James's account and she was practically skint and needed to find some kind of work, pronto.

Most of her gear was packed. Tomorrow she would make sure Andreo's home was pristine, write a brief note explaining that she was off for pastures new, pick up her cases, lock the door behind her and post the key back through the letter box and walk away.

It was for the best.

So she wouldn't let herself cry. She would not!

To hang around, loving him, growing more dependent on him with each day that passed, would flay her.

Andreo Pascali, the volatile, restless high-flyer didn't do commitment.

If he was still interested he might suggest an affair. Which would last until someone more glamorous and exciting came on the scene. About a couple of weeks, if she was lucky!

A hopeless case where he was concerned, she simply couldn't trust herself to say no. She could just see herself weakly complying, getting clingy and pathetic, desperately hoping that the leopard had magically changed his spots and that the affair would turn into a loving lifelong relationship, all the while knowing in her heart of hearts that it wouldn't happen.

There was just one more thing to do before she turned in and sought elusive sleep. Feeling wobbly inside, Mercy dried her hands on the kitchen towel and swallowed the lump in her throat. Coming in late this afternoon, she had noticed the red light on the answering machine, indicating a message.

From Andreo?

She'd chickened out. Had gone to her quarters to do her packing. Hearing his beloved voice, the precarious state she was in, would tip her over the edge and she'd end up crying her eyes out!

Now she would have to access the message. Claudia would have had her operation by now. Conscience-stricken, she hoped it wasn't bad news. Feeling mean and selfish for not immediately listening to his message, she walked through into his study, braced herself for the sound of his recorded voice and felt horribly disappointed when it wasn't him, which went to show just what a hopeless fool she was.

'I've got good news, sis,' James was relaying. 'I'll drop by tomorrow evening when you're off duty and tell you all about it. It's good news for you too. See you tomorrow!'

Sighing, Mercy felt even meaner. She'd been so wrapped up in her feelings for Andreo, obsessed by him, she hadn't thought to let her brother know she'd be out of the country for at least a couple of weeks.

He would have been understandably annoyed at the waste of a journey had he turned up and found no one at home as would have been the case if her stay in Italy hadn't been cut short. As it was, she would have to change her plans and hang around here for a day longer.

Which was tough. Because being in his home, touching things he had touched, walking where he had walked, remembering, was breaking her heart.

She remembered the first time she'd set eyes on him, here in this very room. She'd been well and truly smitten from that moment and had spent most of her time trying to assure herself that it was just lust, quite normal and nothing to get in a tizz about because no woman who wasn't actually on her deathbed, breathing her last, could fail to fancy him rotten.

Then she had finally admitted that what she felt wasn't a silly crush which she'd soon get over. She was crazily, head-over-heels in love with him. In love with a man who would never love her back, who just wanted sex with her. It was the scariest feeling in the world.

Walking to the door, her feet dragging, she leapt

out of her skin as the phone rang. For a moment she felt paralysed, then her frozen features eased into a soft smile.

James. Of course! It had to be. He'd want to check that she'd received his message. He was always thorough, careful about things like that, because he did nothing on the off chance. He wouldn't want to waste his time if she wasn't going to be around.

Wondering what his good news was—she could do with something upbeat to cheer her up—she lifted the receiver and gave a bright, 'Hi! Is that you, James?' And listened to a heavy silence, her brows drawing together.

'Who is James?'

Sharp as a knife, Andreo's voice shook her rigid. Before she could untangle her vocal cords Mercy's mind was racing, weaving a tangled web of half truths and calculated evasions.

Whatever his reason for calling her, Andreo had sounded really miffed when he'd sussed she'd been expecting some other guy to call her. If he thought that, back in London, she was gadding about, spreading her favours around like confetti, he would hardly do what she most dreaded and suggest that they carry on where they'd left off and embark on a full-blown affair, no strings, until he got bored and called it a day.

'Well?' His voice, riven with impatience, blistered her ear.

Gathering her tumbling wits, Mercy managed to respond with a fairly cool—given the circumstances—'No one you need to know about,' letting him know she expected him to mind his own business, then continued with genuine concern, 'How is Claudia? Did the operation go well?' And thought she heard him grind his teeth.

'Excellently,' he got out and Mercy felt her toes curl. That slight, sexy, intriguing accent had never sounded more pronounced. It had always made her go weak at the knees and she had to drag a chair out from behind his desk and sit down when he further informed her, 'I want you to marry me. *Dio*—this was not what I had in mind, believe me!' She heard him expel a hiss of breath and her head began to swim giddily as he softened his tone and admitted, 'Because of the circumstances, I had to spring it on you. I find it won't wait until I can rejoin you in London.'

Then the autocratic bite was back, self-assurance coming over in spades. 'This guy you were expecting to hear from—forget him. You are spoken for. And if you need something to do to pass the time, start planning your trousseau—I'd love to see you in silks and satins, lacy little things—'

His voice was seductive and oh, so sexy now. Mercy was red to the tips of her ears. She felt nauseous, hatefully humiliated. She dropped the receiver on to her lap. She couldn't bear to listen to this; it hurt too much.

She knew exactly what his motives were! He wasn't proposing because he loved her and wanted to spend the rest of his life with her. As if!

Claudia desperately wanted to see her only son settled and married with a bunch of children, his wings clipped so short he would be unable to flit from one unsuitable woman to the next in line at breathtaking speed.

For some reason Claudia had taken to her, the woman she believed to be her son's latest bed partner. She'd probed into her background and had been satisfied with what she'd heard.

Andreo had been equally desperate to make his peace with his remaining parent. And with the looming and dreaded heart operation in mind he would have done anything to set his mother's mind at rest, earn her approval for the first time in his life. Even promising to settle down and give her grandchildren.

Dragging in a deep shuddering breath she lifted the receiver back to her ear. That sinfully sexy voice was now describing their honeymoon and Mercy cut across him in a panic, 'Shut up! I haven't said I'll marry you!'

'But you will.'

He sounded so assured, his voice pure molten honey. She could just see that slight sexy smile! Just thinking about it made heat pool inside her, made her tremble, made her shout, 'No, I won't!' and slam the receiver down.

CHAPTER TWELVE

'SO YOU'RE leaving me for the delights of London?'
Claudia remarked drily. Thankfully, she didn't look
as dismayed as Andreo had feared she might. Propped
up against her crisp white pillows, she looked su-
premely comfortable, her bedside locker bristling with
get well cards and festooned with flowers.

'Only for a couple of days, Mama. I've arranged
for Maria to use my hotel suite until I get back. She
can pop in and sit with you whenever you want her
to, run errands and keep you amused.'

Claudia patted her immaculately arranged hair and
narrowed her amused eyes at her handsome son.
'That's thoughtful of you, *caro*.' He was wearing that
well-remembered stubborn look, his jaw set, his fine
eyes brooding on some difficult, as yet unspecified
project. 'Urgent business, you said. Anything to do
with missing your pretty little fiancée?' she probed
unrepentantly.

Andreo made himself smile. He didn't regret telling
her that in Mercy he had found the one woman he
must have been unconsciously looking for all his life,
the one woman he would be honoured to call his wife.

At the time he had imparted the information he had
truly believed that Mercy felt the same way, that she
loved him. Or that he could make her love him. And
the information that her strong-minded, rebellious son
was about to settle down and produce the grandchil-

dren she had given up hope of ever holding had made his mother ecstatically happy.

He couldn't disabuse her now, not while her health had to be still in a precarious state, couldn't tell her that Mercy had been expecting a call from some other guy, sounding pleased and chirpy about it, clamming up and changing the subject when he'd demanded to know who the other guy was. The only thing he knew about the unknown quantity who was muscling in on his territory was his name. James.

Neither could he tell her that she'd turned his proposal down flat and had actually put the phone down on him!

'I will be seeing Mercy while I'm in London,' he agreed, the smoothness of his tone giving nothing away of his edgy desperation, the driven need to confront her and persuade her to change her mind, merely stuffing his hands in his pockets and smiling until his face felt rigid.

His mother chided, 'I can't think why you allowed her to return to London. You should have insisted she stay on here. She could have visited and we could have had cosy chats about the wedding arrangements. It would have been the best tonic I could have been given.'

That there wouldn't be a wedding—not if he took Mercy's response to his proposal at face value—was not something he could tell Claudia right now.

But he was going to change that.

Once he had set his mind to it, he always got what he wanted.

And he had never wanted anything more than he wanted to have Mercy as his wife.

He said his goodbyes, lifted Claudia's hand and kissed it with inborn grace and headed out of the room, his jaw set, his eyes dark with determination.

James hadn't called back to confirm that she'd be around so Mercy had no idea when to expect him. The 'evening' could mean any time between six and ten.

It was eight now. Edgy, she checked the central kitchen table. The russet linen table mats looked good against the pine, the wineglasses sparkled and the bottle of red wine had been opened to breathe—as Andreo had told her it should.

Only she didn't want to think about him. Or about his insulting proposal.

It wouldn't have been insulting if he had truly been in love with her. It would have been the most wonderful thing in the whole wide world. For a millionth of a second her poor heart had soared on ecstatic wings when he'd said those magical words, then dropped like a lead balloon as common sense took over.

He didn't love her, she knew that. And she had too much self-respect to tempt herself into believing otherwise. He'd wanted to have sex with her and she'd been available. At first she'd resisted but her love for him, her need to comfort him, had led to that night of unbelievable passion, love honestly given on her part, sex hungrily taken on his.

As far as he was concerned she was simply another notch on his bedpost. And once the novelty wore off it would be goodbye. A very firm goodbye. That was the way he treated his lovers. And heaven help any woman who tried to cling—hadn't she witnessed such an occasion for herself?

And hadn't he told her himself that he had no intention of tying himself down for the forseeable future, that he would bite the bullet and get married—some time in the very vague and far distant future—to a woman with her own comfortable fortune, a woman who would give him heirs—and turn a blind eye to his occasional wanderings, that went without saying?

Then everything had changed. Claudia's news of her heart condition had thoroughly shocked him. His father had died, still disapproving of him—of his choice of career, his lifestyle, his women. Every single thing about him. Had virtually washed his hands of the son who refused to conform to his dictates. It had grieved Andreo deeply.

That he might lose his mother too, never having earned her approval, had plunged him into a pit of bleak anxiety. Her heart had bled for him. On her own advice he would have used that last evening to talk to Claudia, really open up, make her see that even though he had most firmly turned his back on the stuffy career and lifestyle both parents had wanted for him, he had been right to follow his own glittering creative star and had become someone Claudia could be proud of.

Had he also gone further, settled his mother's mind with the news that the woman he had with him at the villa was not one in a line of casual lovers but his future bride, hence the shock proposal?

She wouldn't put it past him! He was tricky and impulsive enough. And hard-headed. He would have been desperate to set Claudia's mind at rest before the operation, and what better way than to assure her that he was about to settle down and raise a family?

Her own feelings wouldn't have come into it. Marry him and she'd be tucked away—in the lap of luxury, no doubt—left to raise his children, never knowing where he was or who he was with!

An annoying tear of self-pity trickled down the side of her face. She swiped it away on the sleeve of her old dressing gown and grimaced.

She'd been so anxious for the day to end that she'd bathed and climbed into her nightclothes far too early, as if that could make the morning and her necessary flight come sooner—which was a pretty stupid thing to do. But James probably wouldn't even notice. He had tunnel vision and that was firmly focused on his studies.

The hem of her towelling robe trailing, Mercy forced her mind away from the impossible, manipulative, sexy Andreo Pascali and crossed to mundanely check on the chicken and mushroom casserole.

Unlike her, James was tall and skinny and always looked half starved. Their mother had often grumbled that he'd forget to eat if someone wasn't around to remind him. She had never felt less like eating but she would make good and sure her kid brother enjoyed a hearty meal. He could tell her his good news while they ate and she could give him the address of the hostel she'd be using so he'd know where he could contact her.

As she straightened and closed the door of the simmering oven she heard the low distinctive tones of the doorbell and relief flooded through her.

At last!

James.

Only it wasn't.

Andreo was wearing a casual dark blue shirt tucked into narrow-fitting worn denims. He looked sensational. A slow smile curved his wickedly sensual mouth, his eyes a warm glistening silver beneath sin-black lashes.

'I left my keys in Naples,' he told her lightly and angled his lean sexy body past her, noting her shell-shocked appearance, her unusual pallor. 'Early to bed?' Slow eyes took in her robe, cinched tightly around her tiny waist, a tantalising glimpse of cleavage visible between the low lapels. His pulse quickened, predictably, so close to his beautiful, adored Mercy the muscles around his manhood tightened.

'Could you bear to stay up half an hour longer? I would like to talk to you,' he said softly, reining back his frantic need to hold her and never let her go. He would not be driven by need. Falling in love with the bewitching Mercy Howard had changed everything.

Once he would have been led by his impulses, would have taken her into his arms and kissed her until she didn't know what day it was. For the first time in his life he wasn't going to stride in and take what he wanted, use seduction to get her to say yes to his proposal on a tide of helpless lust.

She was too precious, too important for that. Somehow he was going to have to teach her to love him. Earn her love, deserve her trust.

Her heart racing, her mouth too dry for speech, Mercy could only follow on dragging feet when he sauntered through the hall, heading for the kitchen, suggesting, 'I'll make coffee for us both. Come.'

Why was he here after the rude way she'd turned down his ridiculous proposal? Shouldn't he be in Naples with Claudia, seeing her through this critical post-operative period?

Hovering in the kitchen doorway, clutching the gaping lapels of her robe across her breast, Mercy was about to ask him when, his back still to her, he asked tightly, 'You were expecting someone?'

The two place settings, the wine, the aroma of chicken casserole combining with that of jacket potatoes.

'Obviously.' Her voice sounded thick. And dull. Not one hint of the breezy casualness she had aimed for.

He swung round then, his intelligent eyes narrowed as they raked her features. Jealousy twisted like a viciously sharp knife. He would have sworn she'd been a virgin when they'd made love—although how could he be really sure of that? But despite her perceived inexperience she'd been a fantastic learner, a true natural. No way was he into double standards but, *santo cielo!* he wouldn't stand around while she gave some other guy the benefit of her new-found sexuality!

Whether she knew it or not, she was his woman! His!

He made a conscious effort to calm down, cool it, forced his rigid shoulders and spine to relax.

How could he think so badly of his sweet angel? She wasn't the type to leap from bed to bed, was she? Of course not! Right from the beginning he'd found her earnest sense of morality endearing. It made her so refreshingly different from the other women who had briefly and so forgettably shared his life.

She was probably expecting that girl friend of hers.

He took a pace towards her, the gentle persuasion of his smile making her tremble.

'Perhaps you could phone your friend and put her off? With my apologies. I really do want to talk to you about our future, my sweet darling.'

Already confused by the unexpected appearance of the man she loved to distraction, that endearment, the mention of 'our future', sent Mercy into a helpless tail-spin. She stared at him, very wide-eyed. Surely he wasn't about to repeat that hurtful proposal. It had been easy enough to shout No! at him down a telephone, but to do the same when confronted by the flesh and blood embodiment of all her desires and needs could be a very different matter.

If he persisted. But would he? The way she'd slammed the phone down on him would have put a sharp dent in his massive ego. From what she knew of him, he wouldn't forget or forgive a slight like that. She could only be amazed that he wasn't tearing strips off her with his caustic tongue for having the temerity to turn down such an offer from the most eligible bachelor around.

And if he was so desperate to make Claudia a happy woman, earn her approval for the very first time in his life, then he could snap his fingers and have any one of his former lovers only too eager to agree to be his bride.

Her throat aching with tension, Mercy searched those unforgettable features. Sexy silver eyes held her perturbed gaze and the words Why me? gathered in the tightness of her throat but remained unspoken because, suddenly, she knew—or was fairly sure she did.

If the departed and unlamented Trisha was an example of the type of woman he chose to be his short-term lover, then all those others would be bound to be sophisticated and high-maintenance too.

Whereas she would be quite the opposite. To his way of thinking, if he wanted to please his mother and at last earn her approval then he would have to marry and give her grandchildren. So who better than little Mercy Howard? She would make him an admirably comfortable wife. Pluck her out of domestic servitude and she would be forever grateful, humble and submissive, content to stay well in the background, leaving him free to have discreet affairs with the type of woman who met his exacting criteria in the looks and sophistication department.

Not if she could help it!

And one way to help it was, 'It's far too late to cancel. James should be here at any moment. Whatever you want to say will have to wait.'

'You are seeing another man mere hours after leaving my bed?' Andreo exaggerated harshly, his wide, sensual mouth compressed, eyes darkening with furious distaste, his words driving a stake through his own heart. 'From your state of bed-readiness, food isn't the only thing on the menu!'

While the cat's away the mice will play was a come-back that remained unspoken. She could handle his volatile temper, no problem. But she couldn't handle his disgust. She had no option but to endure it now because she had deliberately brought it down on her own head, and had to content herself with a muttered mutinous, 'You don't own me! I can entertain whoever I like, whenever I like.'

His remarkably handsome features clenched and pale, Andreo noted the flush that crept up her slender throat with deep contempt. His heart felt as if it had been split in two with a blunt axe. Hurting.

Hurting. The minx was clever, he had to give her that. Leading him by the nose, making him believe she was different. Wearing her goodness, her innocence like a false skin, slyly slipped off the moment his back was turned. Turning him into a besotted fool, besotted enough to want to marry her!

That she'd turned him down initially didn't mean a thing. She'd taken a calculated risk and it might have paid off. The little witch could read him like a book. Her refusal only meant that he'd renew his proposal, promise her the world, the moon and the stars and when she had him grovelling at her feet, willing to do anything and everything for her, only then would she gracefully accept!

But it had gone horribly wrong for her. No wonder she'd looked so shell-shocked when he'd appeared on the doorstep. She wouldn't have expected him to fly to her side so quickly, not while Claudia was still hospitalised.

No wonder he was a cynic! Belatedly he recalled the time he'd returned home much earlier than expected, had gone to knock her up and heard male laughter issuing from her quarters. He had been so violently jealous he'd vowed to fire her. He who had never suffered a moment's jealousy in his life. He must have been falling in love with her then.

Seething, he wished he had fired her and saved himself this grief. But he'd come down with some virus and things had happened—

With iron control he stopped himself from venting his feelings, spilling out his hurt, the cruel disillusionment. He had his pride. He would not demean himself.

Impaling her with one final, lethally cutting look he turned on his heel and walked away.

CHAPTER THIRTEEN

SHE'D done what had to be done and never in her life had Mercy felt so wretched.

Not even in the bleak times following the deaths of her parents, because then she'd been able to temper her grief by drawing on happy memories, the knowledge that she'd been valued and loved. This type of wretchedness was different.

How long she'd been standing like a lead statue, staring at the door he had closed so finally behind him, Mercy didn't know. Minutes or hours?

Whatever, she had to pull herself together somehow. If only for her brother's sake. James could arrive at any moment. He wouldn't want to find a sobbing lump of self-pity raining on his parade. He had good news, he'd said and she'd feel really guilty if she put a damper on it, whatever it was.

Crossing to the table, she poured a little wine into one of the glasses and swallowed it, hoping that the liquid would wash away the lump in her throat. She had done the right thing, even if it had hurt unbearably.

She knew her weakness where Andreo Pascali was concerned. Had it been his intention to renew his marriage proposal—and his initial soft approach, his mention of a shared future when she'd fully expected that if they ever met again he would look right through her as if the humble housekeeper who had turned him

down was beneath his notice, had pointed that way—
then she wouldn't have had the strength of mind to
say no again.

Lost in thoughts that no amount of logic could
make less bleak, she was unaware of James's arrival
until the kitchen door was flung open. It crossed her
mind that Andreo had been in such an all-fired hurry
to leave her abhorrent presence that he'd not given a
thought to closing the main door behind him, making
her feel even worse.

But James was grinning. He had a suspicious red
mark on the right hand side of his jaw. And Andreo
was right behind him, looking like the cat who had
found the Christmas turkey unattended.

Stunned, Mercy backed against the table for support. Why had he come back? She couldn't bear it!
She was screaming inside with needle-sharp aware-
ness of him, with regret, wanting, hunger and bitter
sadness.

'Your brother has something for you,' Andreo imparted on what Mercy considered to be a tone of rare
smugness.

'You've met?' Mercy whispered stupidly, her wide
eyes at last leaving Andreo and fastening on James.
Her kid brother was looking unusually smart, clad in
what looked like brand new dark grey trousers and a
classy casual tan shirt.

'We connected.' James grinned, fingering his jaw
with one hand, the other reaching a folded slip of
paper from a trouser pocket.

'My fist with his jaw,' Andreo conceded with a
purely Latin shrug.

'Floored me,' James supplied without rancour. 'I

was on the doorstep when he sort of erupted, asked if I was James. Then thumped me.'

'For which, with hindsight, I unreservedly apologise.'

Shooting the incorrigible Italian a frown of censure, Mercy condemned, 'There was no need for that. How could you?' Pattering over to her brother, she peered up into his face. 'Are you all right?'

'Never better. Your boss was defending your honour. Before he hit me he asked if I was James. He thought I was your fancy man, up to no good.'

'You poor love!' Riven with guilt because she had put that idea into Andreo's too impulsive, too volatile head, she stood on tiptoe and placed a gentle kiss on his reddened jawline and Andreo drawled, 'Mercy, you are detaining him; your brother has a date.'

'Gosh, yes!' His thin cheeks flushed. 'I'm meeting a young lady for dinner.' He ran his hands through his hair. 'Don't want to be late.'

'A student nurse he met on the wards, her name's Annie, they have a table booked for nine-thirty,' Andreo supplied, smooth as cream.

Mercy shot a bewildered look between the two men and mumbled, 'You appear to have had quite a chat.'

'Naturally.' For once, Andreo looked discomfited. 'Once I'd made sure he was okay and discovered he was visiting his sister, we sat in the hall and exchanged confidences. At some time in the near future we will have a proper family get-together, but now—' He raised one ebony brow in James's direction and held open the kitchen door.

'Too right! I must fly! Sis—this is for you.' The slip of paper was hurriedly pushed into Mercy's hand.

'A cheque to cover everything you've ever paid into my account. I always felt rotten about you insisting on supporting me and going without stuff yourself. Now I can pay it all back.' And, as Mercy's mouth dropped open and stayed that way, he gabbled, clearly anxious to be on his way, 'Remember the Premium Bonds Dad bought for me when I was born? Well, believe it or not, one of them scooped the jackpot! See you soon—and you can meet Annie.' Giving her a brief hug, he loped out through the doorway and Mercy sagged against the support of the table, her heart fluttering, the cheque clutched in her fingers.

'Forgive me?' Andreo slid into her bewildered thoughts and Mercy swallowed hard. So much had happened in the last few minutes, it was utterly impossible to take anything in properly.

'For hitting poor James?'

Advancing, Andreo pulled out one of the chairs. 'Sit. Before you fall down.' He took the cheque she was in danger of shredding, his brows rising as he took in the size of the amount. 'You must have given him every penny you ever earned.'

Amidst the confusion of wondering why Andreo had hit James in the first place, why he'd come back in a good mood when it would have been more in character for him to treat her with contempt for allowing him to think her brother was the new man in her life, Mercy concentrated hard on his statement, refuting it. 'Hardly. I splashed out quite a bit with the money I earned for doing that advert thing.' Her tone let him know that it was none of his business. Oh, if only he would go away again, stop tormenting her with his nearness! At least with the unexpected repayment she would be able to rent something halfway decent and cancel her place at that dreary hostel.

Sliding out a chair for himself, Andreo sat facing her, their knees touching. Brilliant silver eyes scanned her uneasy features. 'You didn't tell me you had a brother.'

'You didn't ask.' The touch of his knees against hers was inflaming her and she had to summon all her self-protective instincts to remind him tartly, 'You had the gall to ask if I had any elderly, infirm or drunken relatives or illegitimate children tucked away! I answered truthfully in the negative.'

'But you slid away from the truth when you led me to believe you were about to entertain a lover. You didn't tell me you were planning on feeding your kid brother. Why was that?'

Mercy squirmed. It wasn't something she was remotely proud of, but heck, why should she apologise for a deception that had at the time looked like having the desired end result? And wasn't attack supposed to be the best form of defence?

Her face hot, ignoring the fact that initially he had supposed she was expecting a girl friend, she replied, 'You walked in, decided I was waiting for some man—already in my nightclothes—looked at me as if I were some form of nasty low-life and walked out. What did you expect me to do? Crawl after you and snivel and tell you that the man I was expecting was my brother?'

His sudden grin shook her to the depths of her being, as did the way he took her quivering hands in his and said in a tone of admiration that had her doubting her hearing, 'Your complete inability to crawl or snivel around me is one of the many things I love about you.'

Mercy shot to her feet, warning bells clanging in her brain. Whether she'd imagined that 'love' bit or not, he was doing it again—making her go weak at the knees, with about as much backbone as a jellyfish, only too eager to do whatever he wanted her to do, be what he wanted her to be. But at what cost?

Andreo stood too, his fine eyes warm as they locked with the stormy blue of hers, the line of his sensual mouth softening—as if he were about to kiss her!

Mercy hastily retreated to the far side of the table. Ignoring his slashing grin, she clenched her hands into fists at her sides and held her head high. Unused to dealing with half truths and evasions, she was sick of them. She would give him the truth and if she let slip that she was fathoms deep in love with him along the way then she would have to put up with the humiliation of having him either laugh his socks off or pity her.

'I let you think what you did to get you off my case,' she imparted in a voice that was only a tiny bit shaky. 'I may be wrong, but I got the impression from what you said—about the future and stuff—that you were going to repeat that ridiculous proposal.'

'That's what I hoped.' The purr of satisfaction made her skin burn. 'After discovering who your male visitor was, I worked it out for myself.'

Proud of himself didn't come into it! Mercy fumed, thoroughly disconcerted when he smoothly went on to hit the nail right on the head. 'You couldn't trust yourself to turn my marriage proposal down a second time. So you invented a lover to see me off!'

'So what does that tell you?' Her humiliation was beginning right here but Mercy was still determined to stay firm. 'That I don't want to have to hear you asking me to marry you ever again,' she answered for him, stalking over to rescue the casserole and the baked potatoes, now looking unappealingly shrivelled, and dumping them with unnecessary force on the table. 'Eat if you're hungry. I'm going to bed. I'll be leaving in the morning; you can take my resignation as read.'

'I'm only hungry for one thing.' To her debilitating consternation, he had moved to stand behind her. His hands skimmed her waist then slid lovingly over her curvaceous hips.

Mercy went very still but managed a strangled, 'Don't do that!'

His mouth found the tender hollow beneath her ear. 'Why not? When we both enjoy it?' His warm, clean breath feathered her skin and she shuddered, her ability to breathe at all deserting her as his hands moved to rest on the curve of her tummy, easing her back until she was hotly aware of the state of his arousal.

She should move, she knew that. But she couldn't. He was the master of seduction and she was a weak fool, loving him, needing him...

'So tell me—' deftly he swung her round, facing him, his hands tenderly cupping her face '—why you don't want to be my wife.'

Mercy's legs were shaking so badly she had to lean into him for support. More than anything, she did want to be his wife, but not when he didn't love her and looked on her as a mere convenience. She wanted him, but not at any price.

'Tell me.' Andreo eased her head from where it was buried in his shoulder. 'Look at me, *cara*, and tell me the truth.'

Mercy gulped round the boulder-sized lump in her throat and breathily framed a question of her own. 'Before her operation, did you tell Claudia you were about to marry and settle down?'

His gruff affirmative confirmed her darkest suspicions. Despite her best efforts to control herself, a solitary tear trickled down the side of her face and Andreo groaned and wrapped his arms around her, holding her close. 'Don't cry—there's nothing to cry about, my angel.' Always in the past he'd found a woman's tears to be a complete turn-off, a sneaky device to get what she wanted. But with his Mercy it was different. He had this burning, aching need to comfort and console, make everything right.

'This is no place—' With characteristic impetuosity he gathered her up and, barely pausing to draw breath, carried her to his bedroom and reverently placed her on the bed.

Mercy, fighting a rush of hormones, squawked, 'What do you think you're doing?'

'Finding common ground.' He joined her, supporting himself on one elbow, his free arm pinning her to the mattress.

Sex, Mercy translated with a *frisson* of terror-laced excitement. They had been so good together. Whenever she thought of that never-to-be-forgotten night she turned into a quivering mass of lustful longings. But good sex wasn't a sound basis for marriage. There had to be love.

She laved dry lips with the tip of her tongue and trembled uncontrollably when he touched his mouth to hers and murmured, 'Tell me why you pushed my proposal down my throat and called it ridiculous.'

Inner tension shooting through the roof, Mercy was fighting the hot excitement that had taken possession of her treacherous body. He had untied the belt of her old robe to display the oyster-coloured silk and lace confection Carly had persuaded her to buy on that make-over shopping spree. And from the heightened colour that accentuated the hard slash of his high cheekbones, the tiny muscle that jerked at the side of his jaw, Andreo very much liked the lush curves beneath the flimsy packaging.

Fighting a battle with her natural responses, desperately trying to ignore the tightening of her nipples, the throbbing heat that flooded her tingling body, wasn't exactly helping her need to stay cool, calm and collected and spell out her excellent reasons clearly and concisely.

But she had to try. Right now. Before she weakly melted into his arms and begged him to make love to her because she needed him more than she'd ever needed anything in her life.

Dragging a deep breath into lungs that already felt at bursting point, she squirmed up against the pillows, tugging the parted edges of her robe back together again.

Despite her tongue sticking to the roof of her dry mouth, Mercy managed, 'I won't be a convenience.'

'Explain.' That so seductive smile vanished. His

mouth twisted. 'Knowing you, I could understand that statement had I invited you to enter into a brief affair. Sex and nothing else.' His eyes darkened as they probed her unsteady gaze. '*Madonna mia!* I am asking you to be my wife!'

The abrupt change from dangerous seduction to outraged Italian male pride was like having a bucket of icy water tipped over her head. Trying her hardest not to feel such a sense of loss, she muttered, 'Same thing.' And before he could get on his high horse again she reminded, 'You once told me you wouldn't marry for years, and when you did—for the sake of an heir, what else?—you'd pick someone with loads of money of her own. So why me?'

Warming to her theme, outraged that he should have made her lose her wits and fall in love with him, when she'd promised herself it would be the last thing she would ever do—and hurting herself horribly in the process, she stiffened her spine and ploughed on. 'I'll tell you! Your parents never approved of you and you were shattered, felt really guilty when your father died. Faced with Claudia's heart condition and her coming operation, you were determined to earn her approval at last, weren't you? So you told her you were ready to settle down, marry, give her grandchildren. Well, didn't you? You hadn't asked me, but hey, I'd be a pushover. It didn't matter that I wouldn't come draped in old money. A bonus in one way. I'd be low-maintenance and so grateful—impoverished domestic servant marrying a seriously wealthy high-flyer—wow, lucky old me!—that I'd keep my mouth buttoned and sit at home knitting baby clothes while you carried on your cynical affairs with all those bimbos you seem to find so necessary.'

Running out of steam, she felt her mouth wobble.

He now knew that she'd seen right through him.

Now was the moment for him to whip to his feet, get all dignified and walk out.

But he did no such thing.

He leaned forward and brushed a light kiss across her soft mouth. '*Mi amore*, how you must love me!'

A shiver trickled down her spine and all the way back up again. She'd gone and given herself away. But how?

He told her.

Softly kissing her eyelids over emotional tears, he murmured, 'Having manufactured that amazing scenario any sensible woman in your position would have jumped at my proposal for the life of ease and luxury it offered. A little thing like love wouldn't have rated a second thought.'

His lips moved to her throat and found the frantic pulse beat. 'But you, *mia bella*, are different. It all adds up now. Only a woman such as you, in love and rating being loved in return higher than a world full of luxury and security, would have shouted, No! and slammed the phone down without hesitation. Because you couldn't trust yourself to listen to my voice a moment longer in case I persuaded you to allow yourself to be a wife of convenience—which would inevitably break your tender heart.'

A long-fingered tanned hand had parted the bulky lapels of her unglamorous robe, allowing his mouth access to the tingling spot where the silk and lace dipped between her swollen breasts.

Mercy gasped as a flock of butterflies invaded her tummy, clenching her hands until the knuckles showed white to stop herself from running them through that silky black hair. This was so awful. This battle with herself. Knowing that he had discovered her secret, giving him power over her, dramatically increasing her vulnerability.

He raised his head again, which made her feel horribly bereft until he fixed her troubled eyes with a lambent silver gaze, eyes she could happily drown in. 'You panicked when I immediately flew to be with you, and let me believe you were waiting for a lover. Not once did you give me the chance to tell you how very much I adore you.'

Mercy's heart lurched painfully. 'You're just saying what you think I want to hear.'

'If I didn't mean it, more than anything I've ever meant, would I have acted like a maniac, been so crazed with hurt and jealousy that I floored the first guy who answered to the name of James? If I'd wanted a wife of convenience in a hurry to please my parent I would have closed my eyes to your—peccadillo—and set about persuading you that you'd enjoy a life of financial security if you did me a favour and married me.'

'You were jealous?' Mercy uttered, stunned. Or simply angry enough over her seeming to prefer some other guy to him to turn violent? 'I bet you told all those other women you adored them too,' she muttered, eyes downcast, 'and I bet you don't stay faithful for more than a couple of weeks.'

'Look at me.' A lean finger beneath her chin made sure she did. 'I swear on my life I have never loved before, or told any woman that I did. And loving you has changed me. I will stay as faithful as an adoring old dog, be your slave for life,' he vowed extravagantly. 'And if you think I decided to marry to please Claudia, you have never been more wrong. I told her because I was sure you felt the same way. I had never felt so happy. I told her because falling in love had never happened to me before and I was incapable of keeping it to myself. I actually expected her to come down on me like a ton of bricks, demand to know why I wanted to wed my housekeeper, ask to see your pedigree and your bank account. In fact, far from pleasing her, I truly believed I was about to blot my copybook—in her eyes—yet again. I wasn't to know, at that moment, that she had taken a huge shine to you.' His beautiful mouth softened. 'Though I should have done. What person in their right mind could fail to love you?'

Mercy blinked and swallowed hard. He did love her! He meant it! He had even risked getting further into Claudia's black books because of loving her! She wondered if she could hear a heavenly choir, or was it just her own heart singing? On a gasp of near delirium she wound her arms around his neck and gazed deep into his eyes. 'When did you know? That you loved me?'

'Quit talking! I want to kiss you!' And he did. Magnificently. Dextrously removing his clothing as he did, before doing the same for her, punctuating his efforts with the huskily delivered information she was dying to hear. 'It sort of grew on me. I amazed myself because you were the first woman who had never bored me. You amused me, infuriated me, but you never bored me. Then I started wanting you. And it grew. And grew until I fell for you like a ton of bricks.' He smoothed an appreciative hand over her full breasts. 'This is always how I'll want you. Naked and willing in my bed.'

'More than willing,' Mercy agreed on a responsive gasp, reaching up to run her eager hands over the breadth of his superb shoulders.

He gave her the wicked smile that always made her heart flip and imparted with sexy satisfaction, 'I know you are, *amata mia*. I knew it that time when I was ill and you got in bed with me to keep me warm and I let you believe I was delirious and didn't remember a thing,' he supplied. 'I was at my most devious. I remembered every moment. And I guessed you were appalled by your behaviour. Nicely brought up vicars' daughters don't do one-night stands. That was when I decided that having an affair with my housekeeper wouldn't be such a bad idea. Not when I could see it lasting well into the future.'

'So you made me go to Italy with you! Of all the cunning, scheming—'

Laying a finger over her mouth to silence her, he confessed, 'That was when I knew I wanted it to last a lifetime. And, looking back, I believe I started to fall in love with you when I was spitting mad with jealousy when I heard a man in your room when you'd asked if you could invite a girl friend over. Who was he? James?'

Dizzy with knowing that her fantastic Andreo did love her, with the adoring intensity of his eyes, Mercy struggled to remember the incident. 'Wow!' She dimpled, her bright eyes teasing. 'Oh, that man! Let me think—' Then, because she couldn't bear him to suffer even the tiniest doubt, she relented, kissed the side of his bronzed throat and confessed. 'That would have been Darren, my friend Carly's intended. I was miffed when she brought him with her because I meant to ask her advice over how to get over my infatuation for you, only I couldn't with him around.'

'Thank heaven for that!' Tenderly, he kissed the seductive pout of her mouth. 'Stay infatuated.'

'I'll do much better than that,' she promised, knowing she would never say a truer word. 'I'll be madly in love with you for as long as I have breath in my body.'

'*Amata mia*—how do I deserve such an angel?' He kissed her with driven passion and at her shudder of deep response promised extravagantly, 'I will never look at another woman—how could I when you are all I could ever want? And I will change. I will not leave my socks all over the floor for you to pick up. I will be stolid and staid and comfortable to be around and—'

'Heaven forbid!' Mercy ignited as he dipped his head to taste her nipples, just about managing, 'Stolid and staid would bore the pants off me!'

He lifted his head for a moment, that sexy smile all too evident. 'In that case I could bore for Italy!'

After that no more was said for quite some considerable time.

Rome. The city of magic. Candles glittered on the table in the most sought after area of one of the most exclusive restaurants in the city and the most handsome man in the world was seated opposite, his eyes dark with devotion.

'Happy first anniversary, *mi adorata*.' Waving the waiter with the menus away, Andreo slid a slim case over the table top. His eyes smiled into hers. 'Open it.'

For a moment, unable to take her eyes from his, Mercy's fingers stroked the creamy kid. She loved him so much. The past year had been magical. He hadn't changed much, and then only in the best possible ways. He was still as impetuous, whisking her off to exotic locations at the drop of a hat because there was something he thought she had to see—in this case the ruins of Ostia Antica—and he was still as untidy, but hey, hadn't he hired a new housekeeper, the sensible and settled widow Gray to help her pick up his socks and keep their home spotless? He was still the creative genius behind the Pascali Ad Agency, but he'd delegated the day-to-day running so that he could spend his time with her.

'Open it,' he repeated softly, his smile rocking her to her soul as always.

'It's beautiful!'

Rising, he came to stand behind her, fastening the fine golden chain with its teardrop diamond around her throat. The backs of his fingers brushed across her nape, sending a *frisson* of delight down her spine and she turned her head, lifting her face for his kiss.

'My gift for you is too well packaged for you to open right now,' she told him, dimpling, as he retook his seat. 'But you're going to like it.'

'Oh?' An ebony brow quirked. He loved it when

she teased him. He adored everything about her. 'Do I have three guesses?'

She'd had the confirmation she'd been waiting for a short time before he'd sprung the Rome trip on her. He would be over the moon. They'd often talked about the family they meant to have, had made plans. They'd move to the country, a large house with huge gardens and stables, and a nanny to help out—

He was leaning back, one arm hooked over the back of his chair, at ease, indulgent. The desire to tease him, just a little, flew out of her head.

'In around seven months' time the two of us will be three.'

A beat of stillness and then his radiant smile, his, 'My angel—how I love you!'

He reached for her hands across the table, lifted them and kissed the backs of her fingers, his silver eyes flooded with tenderness, his voice thick as he asked, 'Are you very hungry or shall we return to the hotel and ask for room service if we feel the need?'

'Room service, please.'

He was still holding her hands as if he couldn't bear to break contact. They rose in unison, oblivious to the grins of the hovering waiters. Slipping an arm around her still tiny waist as he escorted her out, Andreo said huskily, 'I have an urgent need to inspect the packaging of the best gift you could give me!'

A Special Offer from

HARLEQUIN *Presents*

This August, purchase 6 Harlequin Presents books and get these THREE books for FREE!

ONE NIGHT WITH THE TYCOON
by Lee Wilkinson

IN THE MILLIONAIRE'S POSSESSION
by Sara Craven

THE MILLIONAIRE'S MARRIAGE CLAIM
by Lindsay Armstrong

To receive your THREE FREE BOOKS, send us 6 (six) proofs of purchase from August Harlequin Presents books to the addresses below.

In the U.S.:
Presents Free Book Offer
P.O. Box 9057
Buffalo, NY
14269-9057

In Canada:
Presents Free Book Offer
P.O. Box 622
Fort Erie, ON
L2A 5X3

- -

Name (PLEASE PRINT)

Address   Apt. #

City   State/Prov.   Zip/Postal Code
098 KKJ DXJN

To receive your THREE FREE BOOKS (Retail value: $13.50 U.S./$15.75 CAN.) complete the above form. Mail it to us with 6 (six) proofs of purchase, which can be found in all Harlequin Presents books in August 2006. Requests must be postmarked no later than September 30, 2006. Please allow 4–6 weeks for delivery. Offer valid in Canada and the U.S. only. While quantities last. Offer limited to one per household.

Presents Free Book Offer
PROOF OF PURCHASE
HPPOPAUG06

www.eHarlequin.com

Dinner at 8...
Don't be late!

He's suave and sophisticated,
He's undeniably charming.
And above all, he treats her like a lady.

But don't be fooled....

Beneath the tux, there's a primal passionate
lover, who's determined to make her his!

Wined, dined and swept away by a British billionaire!

uNcut

Even more passion for your reading pleasure...

Escape into a world of intense passion and scorching
romance! You'll find the drama, the emotion, the
international settings and happy endings that you've
always loved in Harlequin Presents. But we've turned up
the thermostat just a little, so that the relationships really
sizzle.... Careful, they're almost too hot to handle!

This September, in

TAKEN FOR
HIS PLEASURE
by Carol Marinelli

(#2566)...

Sasha ran out on millionaire Gabriel Cabrini—
and he has never forgiven her. Now he wants
revenge.... But Sasha is determined not to
surrender again, no matter how persuasive
he may be....

**Also look for MASTER OF PLEASURE (#2571)
by bestselling author Penny Jordan.
Coming in October!**

www.eHarlequin.com

HPUC0906

If you enjoyed what you just read,
then we've got an offer you can't resist!

Take 2 bestselling love stories FREE!

Plus get a FREE surprise gift!

Clip this page and mail it to Harlequin Reader Service®

IN U.S.A.
3010 Walden Ave.
P.O. Box 1867
Buffalo, N.Y. 14240-1867

IN CANADA
P.O. Box 609
Fort Erie, Ontario
L2A 5X3

YES! Please send me 2 free Harlequin Presents® novels and my free surprise gift. After receiving them, if I don't wish to receive anymore, I can return the shipping statement marked cancel. If I don't cancel, I will receive 6 brand-new novels every month, before they're available in stores! In the U.S.A., bill me at the bargain price of $3.80 plus 25¢ shipping & handling per book and applicable sales tax, if any*. In Canada, bill me at the bargain price of $4.47 plus 25¢ shipping & handling per book and applicable taxes**. That's the complete price and a savings of at least 10% off the cover prices—what a great deal! I understand that accepting the 2 free books and gift places me under no obligation ever to buy any books. I can always return a shipment and cancel at any time. Even if I never buy another book from Harlequin, the 2 free books and gift are mine to keep forever.

106 HDN DZ7Y
306 HDN DZ7Z

Name	(PLEASE PRINT)	
Address	Apt.#	
City	State/Prov.	Zip/Postal Code

Not valid to current Harlequin Presents® subscribers.

Want to try two free books from another series?
Call 1-800-873-8635 or visit www.morefreebooks.com.

* Terms and prices subject to change without notice. Sales tax applicable in N.Y.
** Canadian residents will be charged applicable provincial taxes and GST.
   All orders subject to approval. Offer limited to one per household.
   ® are registered trademarks owned and used by the trademark owner and or its licensee.

PRES04R   ©2004 Harlequin Enterprises Limited

She's in his bedroom,
but he can't buy her love....

Showered with diamonds,
draped in exquisite lingerie,
whisked around the world...

The ultimate fantasy becomes a reality
in Harlequin Presents!

When Nora Lang acquires some business
information that top tycoon Blake Macleod
can't risk being leaked, he must keep Nora
in his sight.... He'll make love to her for
the whole weekend!

MISTRESS FOR A WEEKEND
by Susan Napier

Book #2569,

on sale September 2006

www.eHarlequin.com

HPMTM0906

HARLEQUIN *Presents*

Men who can't be tamed...or so they think!

If you love strong, commanding men—you'll love this brand-new miniseries. Meet the guy who breaks the rules to get exactly what he wants, because he is...

HARD-EDGED AND HANDSOME
He's the man who's impossible to resist...

RICH AND RAKISH
*He's got everything—and needs nobody...
until he meets one woman....*

RUTHLESS!
*In his pursuit of passion;
in his world the winner takes all!*

Brought to you by your favorite Harlequin Presents authors!

THE RANIERI BRIDE by Michelle Reid
#2564, on sale September 2006

HOLLYWOOD HUSBAND, CONTRACT WIFE
by Jane Porter
#2574, on sale October 2006

---

www.eHarlequin.com   HPRUTH0906